JESSICA BECK
THE DONUT MYSTERIES, BOOK 56
STICKY STEAL

Donut Mystery 56 STICKY STEAL
Copyright © 2022 by Jessica Beck
All rights reserved
First edition: 2022

Recipes included in this book are to be recreated at the reader's own risk. The author is not responsible for any damage, medical or otherwise, created as a result of reproducing these recipes. It is the responsibility of the reader to ensure that none of the ingredients are detrimental to their health, and the author will not be held liable in any way for any problems that might arise from following the included recipes.

The First Time Ever Published!
The 56th Donuts Mystery
STICKY STEAL

Jessica Beck is the *New York Times* Bestselling Author of the Donut
Mysteries, the Cast Iron Cooking Mysteries, the Classic Diner Mysteries, the Ghost Cat Cozy Mysteries, and many more.

A HEALTH INSPECTOR wanting payola from local restaurants in exchange for a good rating is murdered. He failed not only Suzanne's donut shop but also Barton's new place, Napoli's Italian restaurant, and others. Suzanne and Grace must find the killer, or everyone could be ruined!

To P and E,
My pair of shining lights!
And to all of my dear readers,
Thanks for being patient!

Chapter 1

"EXCUSE ME? WHAT DID you just say?" I asked the new health inspector after he finished his initial tour of my shop, Donut Hearts. "Did you honestly just tell me that if I don't pay you under the table, you're going to fail my donut shop and shut me down?"

"You misunderstood me," Mitchell Willis said a bit huffily. The man was barely over five and a half feet tall, but if he weighed less than two hundred and fifty pounds, I would have been amazed. "All I said was that as the new health inspector in this area, I have a more demanding set of requirements than my predecessor. I am willing to help you achieve a decent rating, on my own time, so naturally I need to be compensated for my efforts on your behalf. I can assure you, it's all perfectly aboveboard. I will need a down payment on my services by the end of business today unless you want this rather unfavorable report filed tomorrow morning. Feel free to make the check out to CASH, and I'll take it from there."

"Do me a favor and go bark at the moon," I told him icily, doing my best to keep my temper.

If he was upset by my refusal to comply with his blackmail attempt, he didn't show it. "Ms. Hart, I understand that you feel disappointed by your failure to meet my standards, but that's no reason to let your donut shop be closed until you can comply with my list of issues that need to be remedied before I can allow you to reopen to the public."

"All I'm feeling right now is murderous towards you," I told him as Emma walked into the kitchen of the donut shop that, up until that moment, I'd run without a single complaint from the health department in the past.

"Take a breath and do yourself a favor. Think about it before you do something you regret," Willis said as he started for the door. "Remember, I don't have to file my report until eight a.m. tomorrow. If you have a change of heart between now and then, contact me at the number on the card I gave you. It has my home telephone number on it, and I'll be available to you, at least up until tomorrow morning."

I tore the card he'd given me in half and then in half again until it was too small for me to rip again. "That's what I think of your business card," I said as I reached for a heavy steel donut cutter with sharp edges. "Now here's what I think of you."

Willis smiled a bit fearfully, tipped a hat he wasn't wearing, nodded toward Emma, and then walked out of my shop before I could show him exactly what I had in mind.

"What was that all about?" Emma asked me after the vile little man was gone.

"That's the new health inspector for our area," I told her. "He just tried to blackmail me for a passing score, if you can believe that."

She looked shocked by the very idea. "You're kidding."

I hefted the cutter again before putting it back on the counter. "Emma, did I *look* like I was kidding a minute ago?"

"What are you going to do?" Emma asked me.

"I'm going to go talk to the mayor," I answered.

"The health department isn't under his control," my assistant reminded me as I started for the door. "It's part of the County Administration. Do you have pull with anyone there?"

"Why would you need pull with the County Health Department?" Jake Bishop—my husband, who happened to be a former state police inspector—asked as he walked into the kitchen. "Shouldn't you be locking up? I thought we had plans to have lunch together today."

I looked at the clock and saw that he was right. "Sorry. I got distracted."

"Enough to forget you were eating with me? Wow, that must have been something really serious," he said with a slight smile.

"The health inspector was just here," I said, not returning it. "He threatened to fail Donut Hearts and shut me down if I didn't pay him a bribe by eight a.m. tomorrow."

Jake studied me for a moment to see if it was some kind of bad joke, but when he realized that I was deadly serious, his face got red. "That is unbelievable. Suzanne, you and Emma keep this place immaculately clean."

"*I* thought so," Emma said, coming to our defense.

"We do," I assured them both. "Jake, he told me if I wanted him to help me 'pass,' I could hire him as a consultant after hours this evening."

"He actually tried to coerce you into paying him under the table?" Jake asked, his face getting more and more grim by the moment.

"Coerce, extort, blackmail, call it whatever you want, but he tried to get me to buy a good inspection when we already earned one fair and square. What's the difference between all of those terms, anyway?"

"Extortion implies intimidation, coercion is voluntarily giving into someone's demands because of a threat, while blackmail uses the risk of exposure."

"What does it matter what you call it?" I asked him, still having a tough time believing what had just happened.

"It doesn't, at least not until he's charged with a crime. Don't worry about it, Suzanne. I'll take care of it," Jake said as he turned and headed for the door.

"Hang on one second there, mister," I said quickly before he could leave. "Your old connections with the state won't do you any good. He's with the county."

"Suzanne, I don't need any outside help to deal with this weasel. I can handle him all by myself."

I put my hand on my husband's arm. "As much as I appreciate the offer, let me cope with this myself, okay? Don't forget, I was running Donut Hearts long before I met you. He's not going to get away with it, but I need to do it *my* way. I love you, but I don't need to be saved this time, okay?"

That caught him off guard. "I didn't mean to imply that you weren't capable of handling this yourself," Jake said, calming down a bit. "What are you going to do?"

"I'm not sure, but I can tell you one thing; I'm not going to pay him one thin dime."

Emma grabbed a mop. "Do whatever you have to do. I've got this end covered, Boss."

"What are you talking about?" I asked her. "Don't you have somewhere you need to be? Twenty-First Southern is due for its soft opening in three days, isn't it?" Emma and her mother had come into some money through an inheritance, and after I had turned down their offer to buy Donut Hearts, they'd decided to open a restaurant with Emma's boyfriend, Barton Gleason, one of the best chefs I knew, and that was saying something.

"Trust me, I'm fully aware of our timeline, but I have at least a couple of hours to spare before I need to get over there," she said.

"I don't want you to be late on my account. I can handle cleaning up here," I insisted.

"You go take care of this guy and let me give the shop an extra scrub-down," she said. "Think about it. What if you get someone at the county office to listen to you? They're going to want to reinspect Donut Hearts to make sure it's not just sour grapes on our part. Don't we need the shop to be particularly immaculate to back up your claim?"

"You're right. That makes sense," I told her, troubled that I hadn't thought of that myself. "You shouldn't have to do it by yourself, though."

"Don't worry about that. I won't be alone," Emma said with a grin. "I'm going to call in reinforcements and give Mom a buzz." Since Emma's mother, Sharon, helped her run Donut Hearts on the two days of the week I took off, that wasn't a bad idea at all.

"It's a deal, but I'm paying you *both* for the extra work, and I won't take no for an answer."

"That's funny, did it *feel* as though getting paid extra would be something I would fight you on?" she asked with a smile. "Now go. I've got this end taken care of."

"Suzanne, I understand that you don't need my help, but would it be all right if I at least tag along and watch you in action?" Jake asked as I hung my apron up and headed for the front door.

"As long as you can just watch and not get involved, it's okay by me," I told him.

"That's a fair request, but have *you* ever been able to do that?"

He had a point, but I wasn't in the mood to grant it. "Jake? Answer my question, or you're not going anywhere with me today."

"I'll be good," he said. "I promise."

I decided to take him at his word. "Then let's go."

By the time we got to the county offices outside of town, most of the departments were dark and unattended. The county government complex was partway between April Springs and Maple Hollow, so we didn't have that long a trek to make, which was just as well, because I was working up a real head of steam.

The Department of Public Health, which was where I needed to go, was one of those spaces that were clearly closed. "Excuse me, but when will someone be back in the Health Inspector's office?" I asked the jet-black-haired receptionist at the information desk. She was a mildly pretty young woman in her late twenties, with reading glasses hanging from a chain around her neck. Her nametag said Gert Leister, an unusual first name for this day and age, at least to me.

She dug into a large, clearly custom-made handbag with flat metal sides held together with copper wire and pulled out her cell phone. After glancing at it, she said, "Look around. *Everyone* who is working is gone at the moment. It's lunchtime, you know." Almost as an afterthought, she added, "Someone had better get back soon too, because I have an appointment I can't miss in one hour and seventeen minutes."

That was a little more information than I was interested in, especially about Gert Leister's private life.

"Who exactly is in charge of that department?" I asked, trying to get her back on the subject.

"That would be Miss Jacobs, but she isn't here. Mr. Willis is out doing inspections today, but Mr. Ballantine might be able to help you as soon as he gets back from lunch."

I'd already had my fill of Mitchell Willis, thank you very much. "And is Miss Jacobs his *direct* supervisor?" I had no idea how big the department was, and Gert was surprisingly unhelpful for a woman sitting at a desk labeled Information.

If Ms. Leister realized how upset I was, she didn't show it. "Of course she is," she told me, acting as though I were some kind of idiot for not putting two and two together and getting four.

"Okay then, who is *her* boss?" I was fighting a losing battle trying to keep my temper in check, but Mitchell Willis had lit a fuse that I was having a hard time putting out.

"That would be Mr. Simons," she said.

"Then I'll see him if she's not available," I told her.

"I'm afraid he's out as well," she said, though she didn't seem upset about delivering the news at all.

"That's okay. I can wait," I answered as I started to take a seat at a nearby bench.

"Suit yourself, but it will be another four weeks before either one of them are back," Ms. Leister replied. "He's out on paternity leave. Miss Jacobs is his wife. They just had a baby." Almost as an afterthought, she added, "She actually kept her maiden name for business." She clearly didn't approve of that practice, so I doubted there was a Mr. Leister running around somewhere.

"Four *weeks*? Does *anyone* work around here?" I was losing my temper, and I could feel it.

"*I'm* here," Gert Leister said defensively.

"At least for another hour and seventeen minutes," I said, biting back my sarcasm. I was about to snap at her again when Jake put a hand on my shoulder. He didn't have to say a word to calm me down. I took a deep breath and let it out slowly before I spoke again. "And we all greatly appreciate you holding down the fort in these trying times. Who is Mr. Simons's boss?"

"That would be the county commissioners themselves. They met last night, so they won't get together again for two weeks. I'd be happy to put you on their schedule at the next open forum if you'd like."

"Thanks, but I'm afraid that will be too late," I said as I walked away with Jake trailing behind me.

"What now?" Jake asked me once we were outside on the steps of the building.

"I need to see if Willis has gone after any of my friends," I said as I pulled out my phone. "On second thought, I'd better speak to them in person. Feel like going to the Boxcar Grill?"

"That depends. Do I get to eat lunch while we're there?"

In my anger and desire to get to the bottom of the situation, I'd forgotten all about eating. "That sounds good, if Willis hasn't shut her down."

"He might have. Suzanne, can you see *Trish* paying this guy off?" Jake asked me as we headed for his old truck. I'd been willing to drive us in my Jeep, but he'd said that I was too angry, and he was probably right, as upset as I was.

"No, I can't imagine it happening under any circumstances."

"Then let's go talk to her," Jake said. "I mean you can talk; I'll eat."

"I can live with that," I told him as we got into his truck and he headed for the Boxcar Grill. It wasn't the day I'd been planning to have when I'd gotten up that morning to make donuts, but it was clearly what I was going to be doing until I could get this mess resolved one way or the other.

Before I could say a word, Trish caught me the moment I walked in the Boxcar's front door. "There you are. Don't you ever answer your phone, Suzanne?"

I pulled it out and looked at it. "I had it on silent," I told her. "Sorry. I'm not sure how that happened."

"It doesn't matter. Did Willis the Weasel hit you up for dough, too?"

"He did," I told her.

"We need to take care of this guy," she said angrily.

"Jake and I just tried his bosses at the county admin building, but nobody was there."

"I was thinking about doing something more direct, more immediate, and quite a bit more painful to him than tattling to his boss," Trish replied.

"What did you say when he tried to get you to pay for a good inspection rating?" I asked her.

"If you can believe it, I was too shocked to say a word until he was gone. That's never happened to me before."

"I can imagine," Jake interjected from behind me.

Trish looked at my husband in silence for a moment before replying. "What exactly does that mean, Jake?"

I could see that he knew he was in trouble. "Trish, what he was trying to say was..." I started to explain.

She cut me off. "I was talking to your husband, Suzanne, not you."

I shrugged. "Sorry, I tried, but you're on your own," I told Jake as I took a step back.

Jake took a moment to figure out what he was going to say before he spoke again. "What I meant to say, and clearly failed to do so, was that who *wouldn't* be shocked and outraged by that behavior? It's perfectly understandable that it caught you off guard."

Trish studied him for a second, and then she looked at me with a slight grin. "That was a good save, wasn't it? Have you been working with him?"

"I have, diligently. I'm just glad the lessons are finally starting to pay off," I answered with a smile of my own.

"I'm standing right here. You two can see me, right? What's a poor guy have to do to get fed around here?"

"Follow me," Trish said with a smile as she grabbed a few menus.

After she seated us, she said, "I don't know what you had in mind, but Hilda made a pasta and ground chicken soup that is amazing! I've already had two bowls of it myself."

"Sounds good," we answered together. "Does any bread go with that?"

"Fresh from the oven. It also comes with a side salad and a drink," she answered.

"Sweet tea for me," Jake said.

"Make it two," I added.

"Fine, I'll feed you, but then we need to do something about this dough ball trying to ruin us."

"I agree," I said. "Eat first, fix the problem after. That sounds like the perfect plan."

The soup really was amazing. When Trish came by, I said, "Tell Hilda she's outdone herself, will you?"

"I might, but she's been getting so many compliments I'm afraid if I pass all of them along to her, she's going to want a raise, and we can't have that, can we?"

I knew Trish paid Hilda way above the going rate for cooks in our area, so it was obvious she was joking.

At least it was to me.

"If you don't want to tell her, I don't mind doing it myself," Jake said a little stuffily.

Trish patted his shoulder lightly and smiled. "Aw, and to think you'd just about worked your way out of my doghouse."

Jake frowned a bit as he shrugged. "Is it too late to say I'm sorry?"

"I don't know. You could always try," she answered levelly.

"I'm sorry."

"Nope, it's too late," Trish said as she walked away. She couldn't get three steps before she stopped and turned, and we could both see that she was laughing. "Sometimes it's just too easy, Jake."

"I get that a lot," he answered with a good-natured smile.

"So, now that you've eaten, what are we going to do about this sorry excuse for a health inspector?" Trish asked me.

I'd gotten an idea during lunch, but it wasn't fully formed yet. "Did you happen to keep his business card, the one with his home number on it?"

Trish checked her pockets and pulled the card in question out as she said, "I don't even remember taking it from him. We're not actually going to call him and give in, are we?"

"Yes to the first part, no to the second," I told her as I took the card. "We need to get him back over here so we can deal with him in person, though."

"Here in the Boxcar?" Trish asked.

"No, let's use Donut Hearts. You've got customers, and I'm closed for the day. He won't suspect a thing," I explained.

"And then we pound him the second he walks through the door?" Trish suggested eagerly.

"Sure, but figuratively, not literally," I clarified.

"Aw, man, I don't get to have any fun."

"Don't worry, it will be entertaining enough watching him twist in the wind when we gang up on him," I told her.

"Maybe, but I still like the idea of pummeling him," Trish countered.

"Let's call that Plan B, then," I answered.

"It's a deal. So, what are you waiting for? Give him a call."

"Fine, but not here. If he hears the background noise of the Boxcar, he might suspect that it's a trap."

"Then let's go over to Donut Hearts and do it," Trish answered.

"I thought you had a diner to run?" I asked her.

"Hilda can handle the front for a while," she replied. "This is too important to put off for another second."

"Then let's go," I said.

"I'm assuming I get to come, too," Jake said as we all headed for the door after he threw a bill down on top of our check.

"Yes, but remember, *we* get to have all of the fun," I told him.

"Deal."

As we headed back to my donut shop, I started formulating a plan for when Mitchell Willis arrived. He was surely going to get something when he walked into Donut Hearts, but it wasn't going to be the check made out to CASH he was expecting.

Instead, it was going to be something a great deal less pleasant than what he'd be hoping for.

Chapter 2

"MR. WILLIS, THIS IS Suzanne Hart," I said when the inspector finally answered his phone after seven rings. Before I could put the call on speaker so everyone could hear, in the background, a man's voice said, "Hang up that phone! I'm not done talking to you!"

"You can wait your turn. I need to take this," Willis told him, the irritation thick in his voice.

"I said hang up!" the other man shouted, and then there was the sound of a struggle on the other end as the call terminated.

"What was that all about?" Trish asked me. "I thought we were going to lure him here so we could gang up on him."

Jake must have seen something in my expression. "Suzanne, what's wrong?"

"I know that voice," I said, shaking a little at the anger I'd heard over the phone, something very out of character for the man who'd spoken.

"Of course you do. He was here this morning," Trish said.

"Not that voice. The other one," I told her. "Jake, we need to go."

"Who was it?" Jake asked me.

"Can I come, too?" Trish added.

"You'd better not," I told her, answering her first. "Don't worry, I'll keep you up to speed on what happens, but Jake and I need to leave right now."

"Fine, be that way," Trish said as she stuck her tongue out at me, adding a grin to it to take the edge off of it.

"Trust me, you *don't* want to be involved in this," I answered.

Trish was clearly getting ready to say something else snappy to me when she must have noticed something in the way I was looking at her. Her tone softened as she replied, "Gotcha. I'll be across the street if you need me. Call me later, okay?"

"I will," I said as we all hurried out of Donut Hearts and I locked up behind us.

Once Trish was gone, Jake asked, "Suzanne, what's got you so spooked?"

"When I called Willis, there was a man shouting out at him from close by, and he sounded to me as though he was ready to commit murder," I told him.

"Given the way the health inspector has been acting today, it doesn't surprise me. Who was he with when you called him?"

"It was Barton Gleason," I replied. "Jake, we need to get to Twenty-First Southern, and I mean right now."

As we drove to the new restaurant in Union Square, Jake said, "We've got some time, so tell me exactly what you heard, Suzanne."

"Barton ordered Willis to hang up the phone, and when he didn't, it was clear there was a struggle for the cell phone before the call ended abruptly."

"You know, it might not be anything," Jake said, though he was frowning as he picked up speed heading to Union Square. It was normally a half-hour drive, but at the rate Jake was pushing his old truck, we were going to make it there quite a bit quicker.

"Maybe, but you didn't hear how angry Barton was with the health inspector. I've never heard him that upset in my life. Emma's been grumbling about what a colossal pain he's been lately, but he sounded as though he wanted to kill the man before the call ended."

Jake shrugged. "Think about how angry you were when he tried to coerce *you* into paying him off," Jake reminded me. "Add to that the fact that Barton is under a massive amount of pressure with the restaurant about to open. Of course he'd be angry."

"I know you're right, but honestly, I was upset, but Barton's stress level was on a whole other plane," I told him. I was glad no one was out patrolling the stretch of road between April Springs and Union Square. I knew no cop in the area would actually give Jake a ticket, since he was not only a former state police inspector but also a past police chief for our little town, but we couldn't afford any delays. I had a hunch that things might be getting worse by the minute at the new restaurant, and we needed to be there, as though that would somehow make everything all right.

"Try to breathe. It's going to be okay, Suzanne," Jake said as soothingly as he could, but I couldn't shake the feeling that something bad had already happened.

I just hoped that my gut was wrong this time.

"Barton, what happened?" I asked as we hurried into the kitchen of the new restaurant. We'd rushed through the dining area out front, not even slowing to admire the amazing job of decorating that the trio had done on the place. The walls had been painted with some kind of faux technique using rich, creamy pastels that made them look as though they were from the Italian Renaissance and not a local artist's imagination, and the hardwood floors had been polished to a high sheen. If there had been an altercation there earlier, there was no sign of it now, at least out there.

The kitchen looked to be state of the art, a far cry from what I worked with every day at Donut Hearts, but it was only fitting. I was a good donutmaker, some might even say great, but Barton Gleason was a true genius when it came to food.

The young chef was stirring a large pot when we came in, and without any response to my question, he dipped a spoon in the pot and brought out a sample, holding it toward me as though it were some kind of offering. "What does this need?"

"Listen, we didn't break every speed limit between here and April Springs to give you soup advice," I told him, shaking a little from the aftermath of my imagination creating one worse scenario after another.

"Taste this," he ordered. I didn't care for his tone, but it was nothing compared to how badly he'd been treating Emma lately.

I knew him well enough to realize that he wouldn't budge until I complied, so I took the spoon and tasted the broth.

It was amazing. "It's fine," I said.

"Try again," Barton said with a frown. "We both know that's not true."

I took another sip from the same spoon, and then I said, "If I were to change anything, I might add a dash of smoked paprika. It needs something a little earthier."

"You can't be serious," he said with open disdain. Hey, he'd asked me for my opinion, and I'd given it to him. What did the guy expect?

"We're not here to talk about me or your soup," I told him, brushing off his attitude issues. "What happened earlier with Mitchell Willis?"

"That was *you* on the phone?" Barton asked me as he retrieved some smoked paprika from the largest collection of spices I'd ever seen in my life and added a dash of it to the pot, and then another.

"Yes. Barton, did you hurt him?" I asked as I looked around the kitchen for any sign that there'd been a struggle there earlier. There was none there, either.

"What? No! Of course not."

"Don't act innocent with me," I told him, pressing the man. "I heard your voice on the phone. It was chilling."

The young chef shrugged. "Okay, I admit that I was angry, but I didn't do anything to the inspector. He asked me for money, I waved a meat cleaver in the air toward him, and he left. It was as simple as that."

"You didn't happen to use it on him first though, right?" Jake asked him.

"No, not on him," he said a little smugly. "Actually, I should call the man back and thank him. But I can't do that, can I?" Barton asked with a wicked little half smile.

Thanking the man was the craziest thing I'd heard in some time, and I heard more than my share of crazy things in the course of a day. "*Thank* him? For trying to extort money from you?"

"For unblocking me. I was stressed about the restaurant, and when he told me I couldn't open unless I paid him a consultation fee, I lost it, but just for a second. After I screamed at him, I suddenly felt quite a bit better."

"But he left here of his own accord, and under his own power?" Jake asked, pushing the chef a bit harder.

"He was cussing up a blue streak when I smashed his cell phone with my cleaver, but yes, he was fine," Barton answered with a shrug. "It's over there in the trash if you want to see it. It's amazing what a sharp cleaver can do to plastic and electronics."

Jake and I walked over and peered into the trashcan. Sure enough, the remnants of *something* were in there, but I couldn't swear under oath that it had all once been a cell phone.

"You probably shouldn't have done that," I said, feeling a bit calmer now knowing that everything had ended without violence, with the exception of the destroyed cell phone, anyway.

"What's he going to do, sue me?" Barton asked with a hint of laughter in his voice. "I'd love to respond to *that* complaint in court. No, I'm safe enough from the man."

"He could still shut you down," I reminded him.

"He might, but if he tries anything else, he's going to get to know my little friend better than he'd like to," Barton said as he glanced over at the counter where the cleaver rested.

"Okay, I know I'm not a cop anymore, but that sounded like a threat to me," Jake answered. "I realize that you don't mean it, but I wouldn't say anything like that in front of anyone else if I were you, Barton."

"What makes you think I don't mean it?" the chef asked as he tasted the soup again and then shrugged again. He retrieved yet another spoon and offered a bit to me.

It had been great before.

Now it was perfect.

"That's the ticket," I told him.

"I suppose." He clearly resented the fact that I had offered him a valid suggestion.

I was about to ask where Willis had gone off to when Emma and her mother, Sharon, came back and joined us. Emma looked confused by my presence. "Suzanne, what's up? Wasn't the shop clean enough when we left there?"

"I'm sure it is perfect, but I haven't been back yet," I admitted before turning to Barton. "Have you told them what happened yet?"

"No, I didn't see any reason to," he answered.

"Tell us what?" Emma asked flatly.

"I don't want to talk about it, Emma," Barton snapped at her.

I could tell that his words cut her. "Barton, I'm just trying to help."

"You can help me by staying out of my way!"

"I told you before, Barton, that you need to get that attitude of yours in check," Sharon told him. It was clear this wasn't the first flare-up of the man's growing bad attitude.

"What do you think you two would have without me? I *am* this restaurant."

"Watch yourself, Barton. I mean it," Emma said, the threat hanging between them like a cloud.

My husband was about to step in to the ladies' defense when I shook my head. This wasn't our battle, and as much as it pained me, our best course of action at the moment was to stay out of it. As the young chef stared sullenly into his soup, Jake shrugged and asked me softly, "Suzanne, do we really need to be here for this?"

"No, we don't," I answered softly.

As we started back toward the front of the restaurant, Sharon asked, "Do you both have to run off so quickly? I'd like your take on some of our decisions." It was clear she was as put off by the young chef's bad attitude as we were, but she was clearly trying to brush it off.

"We'd love to stay, but we've got somewhere else we really need to be," I told her. "How about later?"

"Later works for me," Sharon said as Emma and Barton continued their private feud.

Once we were outside, Jake asked me, "What's up with that guy and his attitude? He knows he wouldn't ever be able to open the restaurant without them, right?"

"You would think so, but it didn't seem that way to me," I agreed.

"So, was that just an excuse for us to leave, or do we really have someplace else we need to be right now?"

"Think about it," I told him. "Where would Mitchell Willis go after he left here if he were shaking down local restaurants?"

He got it instantly. "Napoli's."

"And how do you think Angelica DeAngelis would take to being extorted?"

"Get in the truck, Suzanne. We need to roll."

Angelica wasn't at Napoli's, though.

Neither were most of her daughters, for that matter.

Only Sofia was at the restaurant, and the moment she saw me, she burst into tears, dropping the rolling pin she'd been clutching in her hands to the floor and hurrying into my arms.

"Are you okay?" I asked her as I stroked her back and held her.

"A fat, wicked little man came by the restaurant a few minutes ago," she said through her sniffles. "Mom and the girls were at the market stocking up, and I was getting a jump on the evening meals when he came in and started threatening me."

"I know. He came by Donut Hearts today, too," I told her.

Sophia pulled back and looked at me a moment before speaking. "What did you do? Did you *pay* him?"

"No, ma'am, I did not. As a matter of fact, I threatened him with a donut cutter," I told her. "I'm not exactly proud of it, but it's the truth. How about you? How did you react?"

"I don't want to talk about it," she said, choking on her words and whimpering a bit as she spoke. That was completely out of character for this spitfire young woman.

"It's going to be all right, Sophia," I said.

"Suzanne, something happened when he was here," the young woman said in words spoken so softly that I could barely hear them.

Jake took a step forward as she backed a step away from me. "Sophia, did he try anything with you?" I knew that my husband felt fatherly toward all of the DeAngelis girls, but he had a particularly soft spot for Angelica's youngest daughter.

"What? No, it wasn't anything like that," she said distastefully. "It was bad enough, though."

"What happened then?" I asked her. "You can talk to us." I looked around the kitchen for the first time, I mean really looked, and I saw that there had clearly been some kind of struggle there. At least that's what the overturned racks and spilled flour said to me. In my haste to comfort her, I'd missed the signs earlier.

"I hit him," she said, her voice almost a whisper.

"Did you hurt him?" I asked gently.

"I don't know," she whimpered.

I was about to press her further when the back door flew open and Angelica walked in with an armful of groceries, accompanied by two of her other daughters. "Sophia, do I smell something burning?" She was about to add something to her comment when she noted her daughter's red eyes and beaten posture. "What happened, child?" she asked as she slammed the groceries on the countertop and hurried to her daughter.

I didn't mind being shoved aside. This was what Angelica had been designed for: taking care of her girls.

"Oh, Mom, it was horrible," she said as she buried her head in her mother's chest.

Angelica looked at me over Sophia's head. "Suzanne, what happened here?" There was a sharp edge to her voice that I'd never heard before, at least not directed at me, at any rate.

"The new health inspector for the county has been going around trying to shake restaurants down for cash in order to get passing marks on their inspections," I explained. "He hit me up earlier, and I wanted to come and make sure you knew what was happening. I'm sorry I was late getting here."

"It's not your fault," Angelica said, her voice softening a touch. She turned to her daughter. "Sophia, are you all right?"

"Mom, I hit him," Sophia repeated, but she wouldn't say anything more.

"She was about to tell us what happened after that when you came in," Jake explained.

"You weren't interrogating my little girl, were you?" Angelica asked my husband carefully.

"Come on now. You know me better than that," Jake said, the hurt obvious in his voice and posture.

"Sorry," she replied brusquely. "We appreciate you stopping by, but I need some time with my daughter to get to the bottom of this."

I turned to Jake. "Do you mind waiting out in the truck?"

"I'm sorry, Suzanne, but you should probably go with him," Angelica told me, clearly distracted by her daughter's fragility.

It was all I could do not to burst into tears myself. I thought we were family after all we'd been through over the years, and to hear Angelica exclude me was just about more than I could take.

"It's okay, Mom. They can stay," Sophia said softly.

"Hush, child. Let me handle this," Angelica told her youngest daughter.

I wasn't about to wait around to be told twice that I needed to leave. As Jake and I headed for the back door, I called out, "You know where we are if you need us." It was all I could do to choke out the words without crying.

"Suzanne," Angelica said, clearly wanting to talk more.

"It's fine. I get it. It's a family thing." I pulled Jake's arm, and we left.

In my life I've been shot, stabbed, beaten, nearly run over, and gone through half a dozen other bad experiences, but I don't think I ever felt worse than I did at that moment or during the rest of the drive back to April Springs. Jake tried to say something a few times to break the tension in the air, but when he saw that I was in no mood to respond, he finally gave up, and we traveled in silence.

My cell phone rang a few times, but I didn't even bother checking to see who it might be.

I didn't want to talk to anyone at that moment, including my husband.

All I wanted to do was wallow in the rejection I'd just experienced from one of my closest friends.

Jake pulled his truck over just outside of the April Springs city limits sign and turned off the engine.

"Why are we stopping?" I asked him.

"Suzanne, I need to know if you're ready to talk to me yet."

"I don't want to discuss what just happened at Napoli's if that's what you mean, at least not now."

"This isn't about that. Well, not directly, anyway," he explained.

"Go on, then. I'm listening."

"I keep wondering what got into the man, trying to strong-arm so many people into paying him extortion money all at once. Something's going on here."

"Does it have to be anything more than he's greedy, and a bully to boot?" I asked.

"Maybe, but why today of all days?"

"You heard Ms. Leister at the county government office. Willis's boss and his boss's boss are on maternity and paternity leave, and the county commissioners aren't meeting for two weeks. I thought it was obvious."

"I get why he might try to take advantage of the situation, but does he honestly think he's going to get away with it when they find out what he's done?" Jake asked.

"That's a fair question. Do *you* have any idea why he's doing what he's doing?"

"I have a couple of thoughts," he admitted. "It was a longer drive back than usual, and quite a bit quieter than I'm used to."

I knew he meant because of my silence, but I didn't respond.

"Let's hear your ideas," I prompted him.

Jake nodded, letting it go. "The most obvious answer is that he needs money desperately, and quickly, too. The consequences of his actions don't seem to matter as much to him at the moment as the driving need for cash."

"Maybe somebody else is extorting *him*," I said flippantly. "Talk about your poetic justice."

"You know, that very well could be it," Jake said in all seriousness.

"I was just kidding," I told my husband.

"Maybe on one level, but it's still a real possibility we need to consider," he answered.

"What else do you suspect might be happening?" I asked him, discounting my ridiculous statement for what it was, an idle bit of humorous speculation.

"If he was planning on leaving his job anyway, and he didn't care about getting recommendations or references, he might just decide to see how much he could squeeze out of clients before someone stopped him."

"That sounds like a really bad idea to me, especially since he just started working there," I told Jake.

"I didn't say it was his rationale, just that it might be," he said with a shrug. "I still like your idea better."

"It wasn't my idea. I was just trying to be flippant."

"Even if that were true, that still doesn't mean you didn't hit the mark. Do you mind if I make a few phone calls?"

"I thought you said that you didn't have any resources in the county government," I reminded him. Then again, I'd just assumed that. Now that I thought about it, he hadn't actually come out and said it.

"Suzanne, I've got connections everywhere," he said matter-of-factly.

"Then by all means, use them," I told him.

"Are you sure you don't mind me butting into your business now?" he asked me before he made his first call.

"This goes way beyond Donut Hearts at this point. Honestly, I'm worried about what happened between Willis and Sophia. We need to do everything in our power to straighten out this mess before things get really ugly."

Jake's voice softened a bit as he asked, "Even after how Angelica treated you this afternoon?"

"I can understand why she did what she did. That doesn't mean that I have to like it, but she's my friend, period," I told him. "If she or one of her girls needs me, I'm there for them. No matter what."

Angelica might have discounted me as family, but it didn't work both ways. She was family to *me*, and that was really all that mattered at the moment, no matter how hurt I might be.

Jake nodded. "Good. Let's switch places so you can drive us the rest of the way back to Donut Hearts while I make a few phone calls," he said as he handed me his keys.

"You know I really don't like driving your truck," I told him.

"Suzanne, it's four blocks. It will be okay."

"Fine, but if anything happens, it's on you."

"I can live with that," Jake said, but after we'd switched places and he was in the passenger seat, he reached over and touched my arm lightly. "Just be careful, okay?"

"Don't worry," I said with a laugh, something I wasn't sure I'd be able to do for quite some time again. "I know how much you love this truck."

"True, but it's less than I love you," he said with a grin.

I smiled right back. "But only a little less, right?"

"I refuse to answer that," Jake said as he winked at me and started dialing.

"On the grounds that you might incriminate yourself?" I asked him with a slight smile.

He didn't answer, but I didn't need him to. I already knew the truth.

It felt good to smile again, but I wondered how long it would last.

Trouble was brewing within my circle of friends, and I was afraid that things were going to get a whole lot worse before they got better.

Chapter 3

"WELL, THAT DIDN'T SOUND very productive," I told Jake as I started the truck and headed into town after he'd made a few quick calls. He'd wanted me to drive while he talked earlier, but I had been too interested in what he might be able to find out from his sources, so I'd just sat there and listened in.

"Give it time, Suzanne. Mitchell Willis is new at the job. Nobody I know has even met the man yet."

"I beg to differ. *I've* met him," I told Jake.

"I meant among my sources," Jake replied. "But don't worry. Something will turn up. I have faith in my contacts."

"I just hope they can come through in time to do us any good," I said as I passed the jail, the clock, and city hall and then turned right toward Donut Hearts.

"Why wouldn't it be?" he asked.

"Well, for one thing, unless I miss my guess, that's the chief of police sitting in front of the shop, waiting for us right now, and he doesn't look happy," I told him grimly.

I pulled into the open parking spot between the cruiser and my Jeep and put the truck in park. Jake and I got out, and the second we did, I knew that my worst fears had most likely come true. Chief Grant, though still a young man, had aged considerably after taking on the job, and I could see the worry lines in his face as he nodded toward us.

"I was just leaving you a note," the chief said. "Since when did you start driving Jake's truck, Suzanne?"

"I wanted to give it a go," I said, not wanting to tell him the real reason I'd been chauffeuring my husband, if ever so briefly.

"What's up, Chief?" Jake asked him, cutting right to the chase.

"It's about the new health inspector," Chief Grant told him, and then he shifted his gaze to me. "Suzanne, did you meet with him today?"

"Why do I have the feeling you already know the answer to that question?" I asked him.

"Okay. Fine. You met with him this morning. What happened, and when was the last time you saw him?" the chief asked him.

Jake put a hand on my shoulder before I had a chance to answer. "I repeat, what's going on, Chief?" Jake asked him coolly.

"You know the drill better than anybody. I need to *ask* the questions right now, not answer them."

"I understand that, but only if something happened to the inspector," Jake pressed.

"Something did," the chief admitted. "Somebody hit the man upside the head with what appears to be a frying pan. You're not missing one here, by any chance, are you?"

"I don't use frying pans at Donut Hearts. How is he?" I asked, wondering if that was what Sophia had meant when she'd said that she'd hit Willis earlier.

"He's dead, that's how he is," the chief answered, and I felt the blood rush out of my face.

"Suzanne, *you* didn't hit him, did you?" the chief asked me, leaning in toward me as though he were trying to put pressure on me.

"That's enough of that, Grant," Jake snapped when he saw the chief's motion and started to step in between us.

"Stay out of this, Jake," Chief Grant barked out. "I have a job to do, and I'm going to do it."

I don't know who was more stunned by the police chief's command to butt out, my husband or me.

"Jake, don't do anything crazy. It's okay," I told him, trying to defuse the tension.

"No, as a matter of fact, it's not," Jake answered icily, never taking his gaze off of the chief of police.

Before things could get out of hand, I said, "Let's all just take a deep breath, gentlemen. Jake, the chief has every right to ask me that question, and you know it. There's no reason to get worked up about it."

"Maybe, but I still don't have to like it," Jake said without even glancing in my direction.

"Do you think *I* do?" Chief Grant asked. I could swear that behind his stern expression, he was fighting the urge to break down.

I knew, because I felt the exact same way.

I decided to answer his question without any more hesitation. "Chief, Mitchell Willis came by the shop and threatened to fail me unless I paid for a 'private consultation,' but he was alive when he left here. I admit that I picked up a heavy donut cutter and I may or may not have gestured with it in his direction, but I didn't do anything with it."

"Can you prove that?" the chief asked me.

"I don't have to. He left here and went to Union Square, so that puts me in the clear," I admitted, hoping the chief of police didn't ask me to tell him how I knew that particular item.

"How could you possibly know that for sure one way or the other?" he asked.

Oh, well. I knew it had been a long shot.

"I just do. Isn't that enough?" I admitted.

"Not in a murder investigation."

"I called him," I said simply. "You can check my phone records and his too. I know these days that you can see where cell phones are all the time."

"Suzanne, that's not enough. I'm sorry, but I need more."

"Go on. You might as well tell him, Suzanne," Jake said softly beside me.

"I can't," I told my husband, amazed by how quickly he'd been able to calm down after the earlier confrontation with the police chief.

"He needs to know," Jake urged me.

"Tell me what?" the chief insisted.

I really didn't see that I had any choice. "I know for a fact that he visited at least two other places *after* he left Donut Hearts," I told him.

"Let me guess. Napoli's was one of them," the chief said.

I nodded. "And Twenty-First Southern was the other one. That doesn't mean that anyone at either place killed the man though, Chief. Willis was going all over the county, trying to extort restaurant owners in exchange for passing inspections. There are probably a couple of dozen folks who could have done it."

"The ones he hit up before you are in the clear, though," the chief said with a frown. "You're giving them their alibis."

"That's not necessarily true," I answered.

"What do you mean?"

"What makes you so sure I didn't hunt him down after he left here and kill him in Union Square myself?" I asked him.

Jake snapped out, "Suzanne!"

"What? It's true, and I'm not going to throw my friends under the bus just to save my own skin. If they are all suspects, then so am I." I knew it didn't make sense to Jake, or even Chief Grant for that matter, but it was a code of loyalty to my friends that was just as strong as theirs was to the law.

"You didn't do it, no matter how much you want to give the chief a reason to believe that you might have," Jake answered. "I was with you the entire time after Willis left here. I'm your alibi."

"You're my husband. Of course you'd lie for me," I pointed out.

"There you're wrong," Jake said, and the police chief nodded in agreement.

"Are you saying that you *wouldn't* lie for me?" I asked him indignantly. Why was I getting so upset about the prospect of my husband refusing to perjure himself on my behalf?

"I'd stand by your side and face whatever consequences there were from what you did, but there are some things I *can't* do, even for you," he answered.

"I guess I can respect that," I told him, knowing how much his beliefs were at the core of him being the man I loved. "Still, I'd be lying if I didn't say I'd be disappointed that you wouldn't help me bury a body if I needed to. At least I know Grace would do it."

The chief shook his head. "Let's leave my wife out of this, okay?"

"Why should we do that?" I asked him.

"Because we all know that you're right," he said with a sheepish grin. "I need to get going." The police chief stopped in front of Jake and offered his hand. "Are we okay?"

"We're good," Jake answered as he took it, but there was still a touch of frost in both men's voices.

"All right then," Chief Grant said, showing his younger age for one brief moment.

"I have one question. If he was murdered in Union Square, why are you running the case and not Chief Erskine?" Jake asked him.

"He's fairly new on the job, so he wanted my help. We're making this a joint investigation, so I'm a part of this mess until we can figure out what happened. The body might have been found in Union Square, but there are plenty of reasons I should be involved in the case as well." It sounded like a stretch to me, but I wasn't about to say anything.

Apparently neither was my husband. "Keep us informed, would you?" Jake asked him.

"If I can, I will," he said, and then he got into his squad car and drove away.

"So, you wouldn't help me cover up a murder?" I asked my husband lightly afterward.

"I guess it all depends," Jake said after a moment of thought.

"On what, exactly?" I asked him, curious as to what that might mean.

"If I thought you were justified in what you did, and there was no other way out of it, I might help you hide it. No, I couldn't do it. If that were the case, you'd get off with justifiable homicide, so we wouldn't have a problem in the first place."

"I'm not sure I agree with your assessment that we wouldn't have a problem, but it's good to know where I stand with you," I answered.

My husband walked over and put his arms around me. "Suzanne, I love you more than life itself. Isn't that enough for you?"

I didn't even have to think about it. "It's more than enough," I replied. "Just for the record, I'd help you bury a body without a second thought."

"That's easy for you to say. The donutmaker's oath doesn't keep you from doing that," Jake answered.

"I never took a donutmaker's oath," I pointed out.

"Exactly," Jake replied, and then he kissed me. "But I took one to uphold the law, no matter the consequences, and I take it seriously."

It wasn't fair of him to do that to end the discussion, but I didn't mind. After all, I knew how much my husband loved me.

But I was worried about my friends and the fact that I might have gotten one of them in more trouble than they could get themselves out of.

Jake grabbed the truck keys from me, even though we were only a few hundred yards from our cottage.

"Don't you trust me to get us home?" I asked him, trying to lighten the mood.

"Of course I do," he answered a bit reluctantly as he offered the keys back to me.

"I'm just kidding," I told him, laughing out loud. "You can drive. I'm terrified something will happen when I'm behind the wheel."

"I get that," he replied, but I noticed he pulled the keys back pretty quickly. "It's the way I would feel driving your Jeep, if it ever came up, that is."

It was a good thing Jake was driving after all.

Before we made it home, my cell phone rang.

I almost answered it, and then I saw who it was. I swiped to decline the call and put it back away.

"What was it, a spam call?" Jake asked.

I just shrugged. I didn't want to admit that it was Angelica DeAngelis calling me yet again. She'd left half a dozen voicemail messages, but I had no intention of listening to any of them, at least not at the moment. She might have been ready to make up for the earlier slight, but I wasn't quite there yet. I understood that her first duty on earth, at least as far as she was concerned, was to protect her baby chicks, but in doing so, she'd treated me as an outsider, something she'd never done before.

Understanding is one thing; accepting is something else entirely.

My phone rang again as Jake pulled into his spot, and I saw that it was our mayor, George Morris, who also happened to be dating Angelica.

I declined to take it as well, since I knew that it would just be more of the same.

"Okay, you're clearly ducking somebody," Jake said as we got out and headed for our front door.

"Somebodies, actually," I said.

"Angelica has to be one of them," he said, thinking about it.

"Very good. Can you guess the other one?"

"It has to be George," Jake said as his phone rang.

"If that's either one of them and you answer it, you're sleeping outside in the bed of this truck you love so much tonight," I told him without the hint of a smile.

It was clearly enough of a threat to get his attention.

My husband wisely declined the call, and we walked inside. We still had a landline, and the message light was blinking on our answering machine.

Jake started to hit play when I said, "Leave it."

"Will do," he answered as he diverted himself from the machine and headed into the kitchen. My husband and I didn't normally give each other orders, but this was a special case, and I felt the need to isolate us from our friends and family, at least for a little bit. I hadn't liked the health inspector—in fact, I'd been openly hostile toward him—but that didn't mean I thought he'd deserved to die, especially in such a brutal fashion. It couldn't have been pleasant for his last moments to pass with a frying pan to the face.

"Do we have anything to eat?" Jake asked as he opened the fridge door.

"We had lunch not that long ago," I reminded him.

"I was thinking more along the lines of dessert," he admitted as he stared into the nearly empty chasm that I'd left in the fridge.

"Unless you put something in there yourself, it's empty," I said as he shocked me and somehow managed to pull out a pie.

"Guess again," he said with a grin. As he peeled back the foil, he added, "The Pie Fairy came, the Pie Fairy came."

My mother had been known to leave us leftovers in the past and even fresh desserts on occasion. I'd resented the implication at first that I couldn't feed myself and my husband, and I'd been about to say something to Momma about getting her key to the place back, but Jake had shut that down the instant I'd told him about my plans.

At the moment, I was happy that he had.

"Strike that. It's not pie," Jake said.

"I'm sorry. Disappointed?"

"I don't know how I could possibly be upset about finding one of your mother's peach crumbles in our fridge," he said as he opened the silverware drawer and grabbed a fork.

"Are you going to eat that right out of the container?" I asked him.

"No, of course not," he said as he grabbed a plate, clearly as an afterthought. "Do you want some too?"

"I'd better, if there's any hope of *me* getting some," I told him with mock severity.

"Hey, you snooze, you lose," Jake replied good-naturedly. "I wonder if there's any chance she left us vanilla bean ice cream."

"Now you're just dreaming," I told him, but I checked nonetheless. "Sorry. You're going to have to find a way to make do without."

"Hey, I'm a tough guy. I can live with hardship," Jake answered as he cut a slab of the peach dessert and microwaved it briefly. After taking a bite, he smiled broadly. "I love my mother-in-law."

"Don't forget to tell *her* that," I told him as I heated a piece for myself. It was truly delightful warm, with the cinnamon and nutmeg coming out in every bite.

When I looked up, Jake was already on the phone. "Dot, you are the best."

He'd put the call on speaker, so I could talk to her, too. "Don't let him fool you, Momma. He was upset there wasn't any ice cream."

Jake scolded me. "Suzanne."

"Look behind the frozen peas," Momma said with a hint of laughter in her voice.

I did, and sure enough, there was a pint of vanilla ice cream hiding out. "Why did you hide it? Not that I'm not grateful and all."

"I knew you would look, and I wanted to make it at least a bit challenging for you, Suzanne."

"It's amazing. Thanks for thinking of us," I said.

"That goes triple for me," Jake chimed in.

"You don't mind me letting myself in?" Momma asked.

"You have a golden ticket to leave whatever goodies you see fit here any time the urge moves you," Jake answered.

"I told you, Phillip," Momma said to her husband in the background. "They didn't mind a bit."

"I didn't think they would," I heard him protest. "I just thought you should have given them a heads-up first that you were leaving it for them."

"I could have, but then what fun would that be?" Momma asked him.

"Thanks again, Momma," I told her.

"You are most welcome," she answered.

After we'd both had some of the peach crumble, accompanied perfectly by the ice cream, I told Jake, "I'm going to go grab a long, hot shower. It's been one of those days."

"I'll be here when you get finished, so take your time," he said as he slumped down on the couch.

"Should I take the peach crumble in the shower with me?" I asked, joking with him.

"Don't do that. It'll get soggy."

"You know what I mean," I pushed.

"No, I can stay out of it, at least until you're finished," he answered, looking a bit like the cute little boy he must have been.

I had to laugh. "Don't deprive yourself on my account. Just leave me a bite or two."

"I can do that," he said as he leapt from the couch and headed back into the kitchen for another portion while I went to take a shower.

Chapter 4

WHEN I CAME OUT OF the bathroom, I heard voices coming from the other room. Was the television on, or did we have company? As I toweled my hair dry, I walked in to find Emma and Sharon in an intense conversation with Jake.

"What's going on?" I asked them as I took a seat on the couch.

"It's Barton," Emma said. From the look in her eyes, I could see that she'd been crying.

"What about him? What did he do now?"

"He's in trouble," Sharon answered for her.

"Mom, we don't know that for a fact," Emma corrected her.

"It's possible, though. Even you have to admit that much," Sharon told her daughter softly.

"Why exactly is he in trouble?" I asked, not willing to admit that I'd told the police chief about his earlier confrontation with the now-deceased health inspector.

"It's okay, Suzanne. I told them about our conversation with Chief Grant," Jake said.

I would really have rather that he hadn't done that, but it was too late to put that particular genie back in the bottle. "Listen, I'm sorry, but I had no choice," I told them.

"We don't blame you," Sharon said soothingly.

Emma didn't respond though.

"Emma? Do *you* blame me?" I asked her.

"What? No, of course not, Suzanne. That confrontation happened, and with the way Barton has been acting lately, it doesn't look good. We couldn't expect you to lie about what you heard. It couldn't have been as bad as it sounded, though. You know Barton. He's got the talent of a top chef, but unfortunately, sometimes he has the temperament of one, too. Sure, the two of them argued. He never denied that when the police questioned him."

"Was it *just* a verbal disagreement, though?" I asked her.

"Barton swears he never touched Mitchell Willis," Emma said.

"At least that's what he told us," Sharon added, though it wasn't exactly an echoing of her daughter's sentiment. Was it possible that she wasn't entirely sure that Barton *hadn't* done something a bit more physical to the health inspector? I would have loved to know if I was right, but I couldn't exactly ask Sharon so bluntly in front of her daughter.

"Okay, then," I said. "Does that mean that you both believe that he *didn't* hit Mitchell Willis with a frying pan?"

"Suzanne, Barton would *never* do that," Emma protested.

"I never said that he did," I clarified. "It was just a question that needed to be asked."

"Well, the answer is no," she said firmly. "We don't believe that's possible."

Did she really feel that way though, or was she trying to convince herself of it by protesting so loudly?

"If he didn't do anything, then why is he in trouble?" I asked them.

"Because of how it looks," Emma said, a bit of emotion coming through with her words.

"We've got the restaurant opening to consider, too," Sharon added.

"Mother, this is not about money," Emma scolded her.

"In a perfect world, it wouldn't be, but I'm afraid that it's at least a little bit about money," Sharon said.

"Excuse me for being nosy, but I thought the inheritance you two got was financing the new restaurant," I said. It was a prying question, but they were coming to me for help, so I thought that gave me a little leeway in what I asked.

"It did, at least at first, but I'm afraid the whole thing has gotten a bit out of hand. I had to borrow against my retirement account to cover the last round of bills."

Emma looked shocked, and it was pretty clear she was hearing the news for the first time as well. "Mom! Why didn't you say something?"

"I didn't want to worry you," Sharon explained calmly.

"I wish I could help, but I'm afraid *I* can't afford to invest in the restaurant," I told them.

"That's not why we're here," Emma explained quickly. "We need you to find out who really killed Mitchell Willis so Barton won't be a suspect in his murder anymore."

"And we need you to do it before Friday night," Sharon added.

"Friday night? That's in three days!" I had experienced some success in the past solving an occasional murder, but I'd never been under such a tight deadline before.

"That's what I was trying to explain to them," Jake answered. "They want me to help you."

"And what did you tell them?" I asked my husband, forgetting about our guests for the moment.

"I told them that it was your call, one hundred percent."

"Good answer," I replied before turning back to the mother/daughter team. "Ladies, I'd love to help, but I'm not at all sure that I'd be able to pull off a miracle. Do you know how hard it is to prove that somebody *didn't* do something? Added to that, you're under a time crunch. Is there any way you can delay the grand opening until this thing is solved?"

"I wish I could say yes, but we need to open this week," Sharon said.

"Suzanne, we're not expecting miracles," Emma added. "Just do your best."

I was about to answer her when the doorbell rang, followed quickly by pounding. "Suzanne, I know you're there. Open up."

It was a voice I was well familiar with, and I don't even know why I was surprised to hear him urging me to let him in.

Apparently, our mayor had not taken kindly to me ignoring him on the phone, so he'd decided to come to my cottage in person.

I had to give him points for persistence, even if I didn't appreciate him butting into something that was frankly none of his business.

"Suzanne, take a deep breath before you answer that," Jake said as he studied the tension in my face and shoulders.

"I could, but what fun would that be?" I asked a bit angrily as I unlocked the door and threw it open. As I did, I said, "George Morris, you need to keep your big fat nose out of my personal business. I don't care if you're the mayor of Whoville, this doesn't concern you."

When I wound down, I saw that George wasn't alone, though.

Angelica DeAngelis was standing behind him, and from one glance at her expression, I saw that she was in at least as much pain as I'd been in earlier.

"Suzanne, hear me out, and then I promise we'll leave," Angelica said. "I know I have no right to ask you for that, but I am, anyway. Please?"

I couldn't shut the door on her. If the mayor had been by himself, it wouldn't have been that much of an issue.

Angelica and I had a different relationship, though.

"Fine. Come in," I said reluctantly. It was by no means the warmest invitation I'd ever extended, but at the moment, it was going to be the best she was going to get.

"I can say my piece from here," Angelica said as she put a hand on George's shoulder. "I was wrong, and I'm sorry."

"Could you be a bit more specific than that?" I asked her.

"You know darn well what she's..." George started to say when Angelica put a firm hand on his shoulder and squeezed hard enough to make him wince.

"You promised to be quiet. If you can't do that, you should go wait in the truck," Angelica instructed her beau. I hadn't seen the mayor cowed very often, but I couldn't even enjoy the experience because of the tension in the air. Once Angelica was certain that George was going to be quiet, she continued. "I came into the kitchen and saw my daughter had been crying. She was upset, and I knew that I needed to protect her."

"From *me*? Really?" I asked icily. I wasn't ready to accept her apology yet, though things were thawing a bit.

"I know. It was ridiculous, and I regretted it instantly, but when I tried to stop you to explain, you wouldn't listen. Not that I blame you. My daughters all made a point of telling me how badly I'd behaved toward you, but they didn't need to. My only excuse is that I was so worried about Sophia's confession to you that I had to do what I could to control the situation."

"What confession?" Emma asked her pointedly.

I wasn't about to let Angelica repeat what Sophia had told us in front of the newspaperman's wife and daughter. "It wasn't a confession," I added quickly. "And you didn't hear *any* of that. Do you *both* understand me?" I asked Emma and her mother pointedly.

"We understand," Sharon said, and Emma nodded in agreement as well.

It might have been good enough, but Angelica couldn't let it stand. "Sophia had a run-in with that horrible health inspector, and then he turned up dead."

I wasn't sure what to expect, but the sympathetic reaction she got from Emma and Sharon wasn't even on the list. "He was dreadful! He did the same thing to us and to Barton," Emma answered angrily. "He went after *Sophia*? That's outrageous."

"No wonder you were beside yourself," Sharon said sympathetically.

"That's one of two reasons we are here," Angelica replied. "One was to ask you for your forgiveness. You are family to me, as dear as my own daughters. Having you upset with me is more than I can stand. Please, please forgive me, Suzanne. I love you."

She was crying, but it was almost as though she didn't notice the tears.

It was more than I could take. "It's okay, Angelica."

She hugged me so hard I thought she might crack a few of my ribs. "It is by no means okay, but I'll make it up to you. I promise."

"You said there were two reasons you came by?" Jake asked, even though I was pretty sure we both knew what the second reason was.

"You need to discover who killed Mitchell Willis," Angelica said as she pulled away. "It wasn't Sophia. I know she said that she hit him, but she told us that she just pushed him lightly, and I believe her. That's hardly deadly force."

"No, it's not," I told her. "I'm not sure why everyone just assumes I can figure out who killed the health inspector. Sure, I've had some success in the past, but I'm trying not to do that kind of thing anymore." It was true, at least for what it was worth. I'd vowed to stop digging into homicides, and I'd meant it. It took too big a toll on my heart and my mind, and I wasn't sure I was up to it anymore.

But could I say no to these ladies I loved so much?

"Could you do it again, just this once, for Sophia?" Angelica asked.

"And Barton?" Emma added.

"Let me think about it," I said.

Angelica knew I would give it my due consideration, so she told the mayor, "That's all we can ask of you. Let's go, George."

"Don't you want to give her more reasons she needs to do this?" he asked her impatiently.

"She said she'd think about it. That's good enough for me."

"And for us, too," Emma added. "Come on, Mom. Let's go back to the restaurant."

"While we still have one," Sharon agreed.

Once everyone was gone, Jake turned to me. "I'm sorry I spoke out of school, but they had to know about our conversation with the police chief."

"You did the right thing getting it all out in the open," I told him.

"So, we're going to tackle this thing, right?" he asked me eagerly.

"You're partway right. I am.

"You, not so much."

Chapter 5

"WHAT ARE YOU TALKING about, Suzanne?"

"Jake, I saw how close you and Chief Grant were to coming to blows earlier over this thing."

"You're exaggerating," he said, trying to dismiss what I knew that I'd seen.

I wasn't about to let him do that, though. "I understand that you were just trying to protect me, and I appreciate that, but I have to be able to push people sometimes, even the chief of police, and I can't do that if I'm afraid of how you might react."

"I wouldn't have done anything," he explained.

"I'm sure the chief wouldn't have either, but it was intense enough to make me realize that maybe you should take a break from this case until temperatures cool a bit."

"Do you honestly expect me to just walk away from the case?" Jake asked me pointedly.

"No, of course not," I lied. That had been exactly what I'd been proposing, but it was clear that Jake wasn't going to agree to that. "How about if you work behind the scenes helping me? I can use your resources and your advice."

"Just not my presence," he said softly.

"Jake," I chided him gently.

"I get it," he said after a few moments. "You know what? You're right. I was so upset that he was implying that you might have killed Mitchell Willis that I lost it for a second. That is not only out of character for me, it's completely unacceptable behavior. We'll do it your way."

"I'm glad you see it that way," I said, the relief flooding through me.

It was short lived, though. "That leaves you with a problem, though."

"Finding the man's killer when everyone he ever met wanted to do it?" I asked my husband.

"Okay, two problems. I might not be helping you, but somebody's going to. If you can't find someone to fill in for me, then I'll have to be a more active part of the investigation, even if you don't want me to."

"Hey, I didn't mean it that way," I told him quickly.

He smiled gently. "I know that. I was just teasing you. So, who are you going to get?"

"I thought I'd call Grace," I told him. "She's been itching to do some investigating with me again, but every time I get myself into one of these messes lately, she's been tied up."

"What makes you think she's free now?"

"When we talked on the phone last night, she told me she's been dying to use some of her accumulated vacation time, and Stephen is up to his eyebrows handling the criminal element in April Springs, so he can't get away."

"Really? Is that his excuse not to take a vacation with his wife?" Jake asked me.

"Don't give me that. I know how dedicated you were to your job when you were with the state police," I told him. Sometimes it was easy to forget that he'd been an active part of law enforcement when we'd first met. On one hand, it seemed as though I'd known him forever, but when I thought about it, I realized that in the course of my life, my time with Jake in it was relatively short, no matter how sweet it might be.

"Guilty as charged," he admitted. "Call Grace, and I'll leave you both to it."

"You're not upset, are you?" I asked him before I grabbed my cell phone.

"I am, but only at myself. I know we shook hands and all, but I need to mend that fence. First though, you have to speak with Grace."

"I'm going to do that right now," I told him, glad that he was going to make things right with Stephen. Not only was Stephen Grant the chief of police, he was also, and more importantly to me, married to my best friend.

It just wouldn't do to have our husbands fighting or even avoiding each other.

"Grace, it's Suzanne. Are you still bored?" I asked when she answered my call.

"You tell me. I'm sitting at my dining room table down the street, trying to think of a reason, any reason, not to do the pile of paperwork staring back at me."

"Then this is your lucky day, because I need your help with a case," I told her.

"Don't tease me, Suzanne."

"I wouldn't dream of it. Well, not about this, anyway. The local health inspector managed to get himself murdered, and I'm on the suspect list of anyone thinking straight. Worse yet, so are Barton Gleason, Trish Granger, and Sophia DeAngelis, along with a few dozen other folks as well. What do you say? Are you up for it?"

"I'll be there in two minutes," she said eagerly, and before I could say another word, she hung up on me.

"I take it she agreed," Jake said as he reached for his truck keys.

"She's guessing I'm here, or she's on her way to Donut Hearts. Either way, it won't be long."

"Good. I'm glad that's settled," he said as he kissed me and then headed for the door.

"Where are you going?"

"Where do you think? I'm going to find the police chief and apologize for my earlier behavior," Jake explained.

"Do you think it will be as easy as that?" I asked him.

"There's only one way to find out. Wish me luck."

"Always," I told him as we heard a car entering our driveway.

"Unless I miss my guess, there's your partner in crime now," Jake said with a wry smile.

"I thought that was *your* job title," I told him with a smile.

"In life, you bet, but you're right. You two are suited for this. Just be careful, okay?"

"When have I ever been anything else?" I asked him, laughing as I did.

"See? *You* can't even say that with a straight face, can you?"

"Not without a whole lot more practice," I admitted.

Jake was opening the front door as Grace swept in. Instead of greeting me, she turned directly to my husband and frowned. "Jake Bishop, you need to apologize to my husband this instant."

"That's where I'm headed right now," Jake said with a quick nod.

"Wow, I knew I was good, but I didn't realize I was *that* good," Grace answered with a smile.

I could see that Jake was about to comment when Grace waved him on. "I'm just kidding. Go on. He's moping at my house about losing his best friend. Go make it right."

"I will," Jake answered, and I noticed that his step was quite a bit lighter as he left.

"What exactly happened earlier, Suzanne?" Grace asked me once my husband was gone. "You know what? Never mind. I don't want to know."

"Really? Is that a first for you?" I asked her, happy that our men were going to work things out before things got too bad between them.

"Hey, I'm just as surprised as you are," Grace answered with a shrug. "Now tell me, how are we going to get started figuring out who killed this guy?"

"Don't you want to know why I'm on the list of suspects?" I asked her.

"Why, did you kill him?" she asked me. It was the same question her husband had asked me earlier, but my reaction was quite a bit different.

"No, of course not," I said calmly.

"I didn't think so. Tell me, why is it obvious you are a suspect?"

"He tried to extort money from me for a passing grade from his inspection," I told her.

Grace looked askance at me. "And you *didn't* bump him off? Suzanne, are you losing your edge or what?"

"Let's just say that I was tempted and leave it at that," I told her, "but when he left Donut Hearts, he did so under his own power."

"You mentioned that Barton, Trish, and Sophia were also suspects," she reminded me. "I'm guessing he tried to do the same thing to them as well."

"He did. I'm wondering how many other restaurants he tried it with. What was he thinking, that he'd actually get away with offering fake assistance for what was clearly payola?"

"Who knows? Sometimes the people with the smallest amount of power abuse it the most," Grace said.

"I understand that, but how did he think he was going to get away with it in the long run?"

"Tell me he wasn't so blatant as to openly ask you for money," Grace said.

"No, it was all disguised as a consulting fee after hours," I admitted.

"I wonder if there's anything illegal about him phrasing it that way?"

"I can't imagine that there's not," I said indignantly.

"Oh, you'd be amazed by what you can get away with at some workplaces, especially if it's in local government."

"Are you talking about George Morris?" I asked.

"No, not our George, but it doesn't surprise me that someone might try to earn a little extra cash on the side. We should speak with his supervisor."

"I tried. She's out on maternity leave."

"Then her supervisor," Grace suggested.

"He's on paternity leave with her."

"So, you aren't exactly coming into this blindly, are you?"

"Grace, I was so angry by what he was trying to do I wanted to get him fired on the spot. Jake went with me to Maple Hollow to the county government offices, and we tried to find out who to complain to about Willis's behavior. The only supervision he's getting at the moment is from the county commissioners, who don't meet for another two weeks."

"So he had a window of opportunity to extort money from all of you, and he took it. I wonder why he felt the need to push you all at once, though? Wouldn't it have made more sense to just go after the weakest link of the group?"

"Do *any* of us appear to be weak links to you?" I asked with a frown.

"No. That's my point. It sounds to me as though he was desperate for an infusion of cash, not just trolling for a likely patsy or two. The question is why."

"That's probably something we need to find out," I told her. "Feel like taking a trip to the county seat with me?"

"I'm game if you are," she said.

"Then let's go," I told her.

It wasn't that easy, though.

We were just nearing Grace's place in my Jeep when her husband, the chief of police, flagged us down.

I stopped and leaned over across Grace to speak with him. "I know I wasn't speeding. I didn't have time to work up to it."

"Grace, where are you going?" he asked his wife, ignoring me completely.

"I'm going to help Suzanne with this case," she told her husband.

"I know you are. I just wanted to see if you'd actually admit it to my face," Chief Grant told his wife.

"Why on earth would I ever have a problem doing that?" There was an edge to her voice that I wasn't at all certain Stephen Grant caught, but I surely knew that it meant that a storm was coming if he decided to pursue this particular line of questioning.

"I'd really rather you didn't, if it's all the same to you. It almost caused a bad rift between Jake and me, and I'd hate to see it have that effect on the two of us."

She leaned out the window and patted his cheek gently. "Don't worry about it. We won't let it."

"So you're going to go ahead and help Suzanne anyway, even after I asked you not to?" he asked her.

"Stephen, I love you. You're my husband, and I'd do practically anything to make you happy," Grace said calmly.

The police chief looked relieved, but I knew it was premature. After all, I'd known Grace nearly my entire life, an advantage he lacked. "That's good to hear."

"But," Grace started.

"No buts. Let's just end it right there, okay?" he asked hopefully.

"But," Grace repeated, "Suzanne needs my help, and she's going to get it." She looked around. "Where's Jake? Don't tell me you were too proud to accept his apology and he stormed off."

"I won't tell you that," Stephen said, and I felt myself worrying about the men again when he added, "Because we worked it out. Hey, I would have done the same thing in his shoes."

"Then where is he?" I asked.

"He's checking something out for me," the police chief said cryptically.

"Care to share what it is with us?" Grace asked him sweetly.

"Not on your life, kiddo," he answered with a grin.

"Kiddo?" she asked him archly.

"Yeah, it's my new nickname for you. How do you like it?"

"I think you should keep trying," she said, and then she offered him a quick smile. "As much fun as it is to sit here sparring with you, Suzanne and I have work to do."

"At least be careful," the police chief told his wife.

"Right back at you, *kiddo*," Grace said with a grin.

"Yeah. That's no good. I hear it now."

"Good," Grace answered, and I took that as the perfect opportunity to drive away while we still could. I was just as curious as Grace about the errand my husband was running for the chief of police, but if the two men were getting along again, that was really all that mattered to me. I had a great many acquaintances and even quite a few friends, but there was a core of people I had around me that I trusted with my life, and I hated seeing two of them at odds with each other. At least I could forget about that now, which was a good thing, since Grace and I had something a great deal more serious on our plates at the moment.

Chapter 6

"IT'S ALMOST CLOSING time for the day," Gert Leister at the county government offices said the second I approached her desk. She looked disheveled, and I had to wonder if her earlier appointment hadn't gone as planned, but I wasn't about to ask her a personal question if I could help it. "I'm surprised you came back."

"As a matter of fact, I am, too," I said as brightly as I could manage.

"I'm not exactly sure why you're here," she said flatly.

"Sometimes I find myself wondering the exact same thing."

"What is that supposed to mean?" To my surprise, the young woman must have caught the hint of sarcasm in my voice, something that caught me off guard.

"I just meant that I was glad that *you* made it back to your post after your appointment," I told her as sincerely as I could muster. "We need to know about Mitchell Willis."

"Somebody killed him," the woman said with a hitch in her voice, and for the first time, I noticed that she'd been crying. "Honestly, the guy was just trying to do his job, and some restaurant owner in Union Square decided to kill him, just like that." She snapped her fingers once to show what she meant.

"How do you know an owner did it?" I asked her.

"Who else could it be? You should have heard the angry phone calls I'd been getting the past days about him. Still, why kill him just because he gave someone a bad rating?" She retrieved that large and awkward handbag again and got out a small pack of tissues. After dabbing at her eyes, she just shrugged as though she couldn't make any sense of it all.

"It's terrible," I agreed. "Were you two close?"

"Not really," she said, shaking that head of black hair from side to side. "He asked me out when I first came to work here, but when I turned him down, he almost seemed relieved. It was pretty obvious there was somebody else he *wanted* to go out with, but I guess she kept turning him down."

"Really?" I asked, clearly surprised by the admission. Mitchell hadn't seemed like a ladies' man to me, or even someone who *wanted* to be one, for that matter. "Was it someone who worked here?"

"I don't have a clue," she said. "For that, you'd have to ask Fred."

"We'd be happy to. Where might we find him?" Grace asked her.

"You *might* find him in Las Vegas, or maybe even the South Pacific, but I doubt you will. He's most likely at Bar None. That's usually where he has his dinner." A timer went off in her bag, and after rooting around for it, she snapped it off and stood. "Sorry I couldn't be more help to you. My workday just ended."

"Hang on one second. Did you say Bar None?" I asked.

"Yeah. The owner *thinks* it's a cute name. She goes around saying she has the best bar around, bar none. I don't go there myself. There are too many strange men hitting on me all of the time. It's a curse, you know."

I studied the woman again, wondering if she might be pulling my leg, but clearly, she wasn't. "I hate when that happens," I said.

"Are you saying that it actually happens to *you*?" she asked me incredulously.

"Yes, even me," I said, trying not to act miffed that she'd implied that no man in his right mind would make a pass at me. True, I was a twice-married lady with a few extra pounds and several more miles on me than I cared to admit to, but that didn't mean I didn't still like to think of myself as a fetching young woman, even if the mirror told a different story.

"Come on, Suzanne," Grace said as she touched my shoulder lightly. "I need a drink."

"Don't we all, sister," the woman said a bit shakily, surprising me yet again. "Tell Fred I sent you, not that he won't tell you his life's story without you even asking. He complains that women love to gossip, but I've never heard anyone talk about other people as much as Fred does."

"He sounds perfect to me," Grace said with a smile.

Gert looked a bit surprised herself by that assessment of her colleague. "If you say so. On second thought, *don't* tell him I sent you. I don't want him getting any ideas."

"We wouldn't do that to either one of you," I said with a brightly artificial smile.

Let her figure that one out on her own.

"I thought she was kidding, but it really is called Bar None," Grace said as we walked into the bar. It sounded like the beginning of a bad joke to me. Two women walk into a bar.... I suppose it was, but we weren't there for our own entertainment or even to have a drink.

We needed to get some information about the late Mitchell Willis so we could help our friends, and if that meant getting close to this man named Fred who loved to gossip, then so be it.

Fred wasn't that hard to spot, especially since he wore his county government nametag around his neck. His short-sleeved white dress shirt was wrinkled, and his tie was askew.

"You must be Fred," I said as I took a seat at his table, where he'd been sitting alone, nursing a pathetic little hamburger that Trish wouldn't have served on her worst day. It appeared to be made from *some* kind of meat, at least what there was of it, but what the exact source was I wouldn't risk a guess. The bun had been toasted to the point of cremation, and the paltry lettuce I could see was barely green. Lying limply on the plate beside it was a batch of French fries that must have skipped most of their time in the deep fryer. They were paler than the man eating them, and that was saying something.

Half-heartedly, as though he told the joke by rote every day of his life, he said, "I must be, since that's what my dearly departed mother named me." He took a large swig from the mug of beer beside his plate.

"I'm sorry for your loss," I said automatically.

"Don't be. She just departed for Cleveland, but I expect her back next week." How many beers had Fred had already? Did he actually get hammered on his way home every night? It was none of my business, but I still couldn't imagine it.

"That's so funny," I said without much enthusiasm. "We heard you were the man to speak with about Mitchell Willis."

Fred looked extremely sad at the mention of the murder victim's name. Almost as an afterthought, he took a small bite of his burger and then washed it down with an inordinately big swallow of beer, killing the glass. "I don't want to talk about it."

Grace said, "Tell you what. I'll be right back with your next drink, since yours is empty."

Fred just shrugged, so Grace took it as a sign that if she brought it, he'd drink it.

While she was gone retrieving his next drink, I asked, "Did you know Mitchell well?"

"He was my best friend in the world, as sad as that sounds when I say it out loud," Fred admitted. "I can't believe somebody clobbered him like that. I heard they used a steel skillet on him." He shivered a bit at the thought of it and reached for the mug, which was already empty.

"You must really be hurting," I said.

"I still can't believe he's gone," Fred said, staring into the bottom of his empty mug. He was clearly feeling the effects of the liquid part of his dinner, and we were, probably not too wisely, adding fuel to the fire.

"We understand that Mitchell had a crush on somebody at the office," I said.

"Are you talking about that thing he had for Irene? It was nothing. Absolutely nothing. Mitchell only cared about one thing, and it surely wasn't a woman."

Before I could ask him what Mitchell cared so much about, Grace returned with his fresh beer and asked him, "Do you know anybody who had a particular beef with him?"

"He told me a few nights ago that he owed someone some money, more than he could get his hands on, and he was desperate for a way to come up with some to get him off his back."

"Like a loan shark?" Grace asked.

"Like one, but without the professional status," Fred said. "Smiley Bonner has been known to run a bit of a lending bank out of his back room at the pawn shop. Word was that Mitchell was into him, and deep."

Wow. That could explain why the health inspector had suddenly been extorting money. "How did he get so far in debt? Was it gambling? Women? Drugs?" Grace asked.

"Orange," Fred said sadly before taking another gulp of the new beer.

"Orange? Are you talking about the fruit?" I asked, puzzled by his answer.

"No, the color. That was his collection, the only thing he ever really loved in his life. Mitchell was obsessed with all things orange, more of them than he could afford, evidently. He was fixated on them. His collection covered everything from traffic cones to hazmat suits to the orange properties in Monopoly."

"How much could those kinds of orange things really be worth?" Grace asked him, clearly as surprised by the admission as I was.

"He told me last week that one of the orange pieces of jewelry, some crazy ring he'd just gotten, was worth over fifty grand. He admitted that he went into hock for that one at the pawn shop," the man said with a shrug. "Go figure."

"And he got so deep into debt buying orange things that he owed an amateur loan shark money?" I asked incredulously.

"Hey, we all have our vices," he said as he polished off the beer we'd bought him. "I don't suppose there's another where that one came from, is there? I'm so numb with pain that I'm not even feeling these."

"I'll get it this time," I said as I approached the bar.

The woman had one drawn before I even made my order. "Tell Fred this is his last one."

"Is he that drunk?" I asked.

"He's drunk enough. One more after this and he'll be sleeping it off in my storeroom, and neither one of us wants that to happen again. What kind of bunk is he feeding you two?"

"We're talking about Mitchell Willis. He said he was his best friend," I admitted as I paid her. "Did you know the man?"

"I knew of him, but he never took a step across my threshold, so we didn't have much contact. Listen, take anything Fred tells you with a grain of salt. He likes to think he knows where the skeletons are all buried, but personally, I think he makes half of it up on the fly."

"Do you happen to know which half we should ignore?" I asked her with a slight grin.

"Sorry, I can't say that I do," she answered, returning my smile with one of her own.

"I was told to tell you this was your last drink," I told Fred as I set the beer down in front of him.

"Come on, Maggie," he said loudly to the bartender. "I'm in pain over here. I just lost my only friend."

She chose to ignore him, which I imagined was a skill she'd acquired early on. I had already discovered that a little bit of Fred went a long way.

"Anything else you want to share with us about Mitchell Willis before we go?" I asked him as I sat back down.

"Yeah. He might not have been a peach, but he deserved better than he got," Fred said somberly. Instead of touching his last beer, he stared into its depths as though he were searching for an answer he wasn't going to find there. "I don't know anything else. Thanks for the drinks." He said that last bit without even looking up from his glass. Evidently, the magnitude of what had happened to his coworker and friend was finally starting to sink in.

Grace was about to press him again when I shook my head slightly. "Thank you for your time, Fred. We're truly sorry for your loss." It was the second time I'd said it since I'd met the man, but this time, I actually meant it. He'd said earlier, whether it had been a slip or not, that Mitchell Willis had been his only friend, and I felt bad for him.

In Vino Veritas. In wine—or in this case, beer—there is truth.

The liquor had shown us his true feelings.

At least that was what I chose to believe.

"He's quite a character, isn't he?" Grace asked me once we walked out of the bar into the bright sunshine.

"I'd say that's an understatement if ever there was one. It's really kind of sad."

"If what he told us is true. The bartender warned me that half of what Fred told us would be pure bunk," Grace said.

"She told me the same thing," I admitted.

"So what do we do?"

"We investigate as though everything we just heard was the absolute and unvarnished truth," I replied.

"Then what's our next move?"

"Let's start with Smiley Bonner, the pawnbroker, and go from there."

"I'm on board with that," Grace said as she smelled the sleeve of her jacket. "I'm not a fan of that aroma."

"Stale beer and cheap alcohol or questionable burned meat? I know that I like to complain about smelling like donuts all of the time, but I don't think I'll fuss about it anymore. It's like a breath of fresh air compared to this."

"Maybe we'll air out along the way before we get to the pawn shop," Grace said.

"One can only hope, but I don't care what it's like outside, we're driving with the windows down on my Jeep."

"Agreed," Grace said.

By the time we got to Smiley's Pawn Shop, most of the remaining aroma we'd acquired at Bar None had dissipated in the wind.

At least we had something to show for our investigation so far.

Chapter 7

"WOW, I'VE NEVER SEEN a pawnshop with so many lovely rings on display," I said as we surveyed one large selection of Smiley's goods he offered for sale. The man behind the counter was bald and clearly older, with wizened features that didn't come anywhere near smiling since we'd walked in the door, belying his nickname, unless it had been given to him ironically.

However, one mention of his goods and his face lit up. "You like these? You should have seen the ones that went out the door last month! Just for example, I had a beautiful two-carat diamond ring with a ring of emeralds around it that I let go for next to nothing not ten days ago."

"Do you have any stones with an orange tint to them?" Grace asked him before I could bring it up. "An old friend of ours used to collect them. Mitchell Willis. Maybe you knew him."

"I know a lot of people," the man said, definitely cooling toward us after hearing the murder victim's name.

"Your real name is Calvin Bonner, am I right?" I asked. Grace had found it online on our way there, so I wanted to use his given name to throw him off if I could.

"Guilty as charged," he admitted. "So, ladies, are you in the market for some new jewelry today or not?"

I ignored his direct question. "We'd really like to know about your relationship with Mitchell Willis."

And that's when the smile vanished from Calvin Bonner's face completely.

"I don't have anything to say about him one way or the other," he answered brusquely and started to move away. "Hang on a second," Bonner said. "You just referred to him in the past tense a couple of times. What's the matter? Aren't you all friends anymore?"

"You haven't heard the news?" I asked him.

"What news is that? It's been slow here all afternoon. Nobody's come in or out since lunch."

"And you've been here all that time?" I asked him. It just might be possible to get the man's alibi before he even realized the victim was dead.

"No, I take off from noon to three every day. I go home, have a bite to eat, and then I take a long nap. I'm not as young as I used to be, and I stay open late."

"And you just lock the place up?" I asked him.

"I've got a guy who comes in and covers for me. Why does that matter?"

Grace ignored his question and his growing attitude. "Do you have lunch with your wife, by any chance?"

"I'm not married. Never have been. It's always been just me," he explained gruffly.

"So, no one saw you for three hours today?" I pressed him.

"Nobody sees me for three hours *every* day," Bonner answered impatiently. "Why does it even matter?"

"Because Mitchell Willis was murdered sometime during your lunch hour, and from the sounds of it, there was no love lost between the two of you," Grace said.

"Murdered? He's dead? I don't believe it," Bonner said with a frown. "That's not possible. He can't do that to me."

"I'm afraid it's true. What exactly did he do to you?" I asked.

"He owed me fifty thousand dollars, that's what he did!" Calvin Bonner said loudly.

"So it's true? You loaned him that much money to buy a piece of orange jewelry?" Grace asked incredulously.

"I didn't *loan* him anything. I let him have more than I should have without securing enough collateral to cover it."

"I find it hard to believe that someone who runs a pawnshop would ever let that happen," I told him. "Isn't taking advantage of people kind of your business model?"

"Hey, I don't force anybody to come in here and do business with me. Willis was a good customer. Every now and then, I let him slide a little on paying me, you know? He was always good for it. Stupid, I know. I should have grabbed that ring back when I had the chance two nights ago."

"Is that the last time you saw him alive?"

Smiley nodded morosely. "He wanted to show me something else he'd bought, so I stopped by his place on my way home from work."

"What had he found?" I asked.

"A porcelain belly dancer about twelve inches tall with a large orange gemstone in its belly button. It was hideous, but Willis acted like it was the *Mona Lisa*. The fool paid six grand for it, most of that value in the gem itself, and we had words."

"About?" I asked.

"About how he could afford to buy that piece of junk when he still owed *me* so much money. He told me he'd have the money for me tomorrow though, and I believed him. Now I'll never see my money, or that ring, ever again."

"Was anybody else around when you went to his place?" I asked him.

"No, it was just the two of us. Why?"

"I'm just wondering if maybe you weren't nearly as nice about everything as you're pretending to be. What if you went to his place to get the money or the ring? When he wouldn't come through, you gave him a deadline, but it wasn't tomorrow. It was today. When he didn't pay up or give the ring back during your lunch hour, you lost control and smashed his face in with a frying pan."

"I did no such thing," Smiley protested. "It's like I said. He had until tomorrow at noon to pay me or bring the ring back. Why would I kill him if I didn't have the ring or the money?"

"It's just your word that you don't have either one," Grace pushed him.

"I'm telling you, I didn't do it!" Calvin protested again. I noticed him moving toward a selection of firearms he had for sale.

Surely none of them were loaded.

At least I hoped not.

If Grace saw where he was going, she didn't act like it.

I decided it was time to pull back a bit from our accusations and see if he could help us with anyone else who might have been responsible for Mitchell Willis's demise. "So, if you didn't kill the man, then who do you think might have?"

"Are you kidding? I could make you a list," he said sarcastically.

"Why don't you do that?" I suggested.

"Hang on a second. Why should I tell you anything? You two aren't cops."

"How do you know that?" Grace asked him.

"Trust me, after forty-two years in this business, I know a cop the second one walks through that door. How did you know Willis? You can stop trying to sell the story that you're all old friends. I know better."

"How could you possibly know that?" I asked him.

"You're forgetting something. I *knew* Willis. He didn't have any women friends," he replied.

I could see Grace concocting another lie, so I cut her off before she could. It was time for the truth. "He tried to extort me earlier today, most likely so he could pay for that ring."

"What did he have on you?" Bonner asked me.

"A passing health inspection," I told him.

"I can't believe he'd jeopardize his job like that," the pawnbroker said with disgust.

"I'm sure he didn't feel as though he had any choice," Grace said, "especially after you gave him that ultimatum."

I had a sudden hunch, and I decided to go with it and see where it led. There was more to this story than he was sharing with us. "You had another buyer who was willing to pay a lot more than Mitchell Willis did for that ring, didn't you?"

"How could you possibly know that?" Bonner asked her, clearly startled by my guess.

I must have been right on the money. "It's a small world, Mr. Bonner," I answered cryptically. "People talk."

"Well, none of that matters now. I've got to get over to his place and look for that ring," Smiley said as he grabbed his jacket.

"We'll go with you," Grace offered as we followed him out of the shop.

"I don't need supervision," he snapped as he locked his door after flipping the sign to CLOSED.

"We aren't finished with you, though," Grace told him.

"That's too bad, because I'm finished with the both of you," he answered as he headed to a beat-up old pickup truck and slammed the door in our faces.

"That went well," Grace said with disgust.

"Get in the Jeep," I ordered her as I headed for my vehicle. "We're going to follow him."

"He's not going to like that," she said as she complied nonetheless.

"I wasn't aware that was a factor," I answered as I hurried to catch up with him.

I wanted to get to Mitchell Willis's place before Bonner had a chance to break in, which was what I was sure his plan was. He didn't seem like all that thoughtful a fellow, and it was obvious that as far as he was concerned, he'd be justified in doing it.

I pulled in beside him after he stopped and got out of his truck, but it was clear that Calvin Bonner wasn't going to get his wish today.

There was a cop standing guard outside of the house where he'd just driven up, barring the way.

"You gotta let me in to get my property," he argued with the young cop as he tried to push past her.

"I don't *gotta* do anything," the young woman said calmly as she took one arm, shoved it into his chest, and shut him down in his tracks. "This is part of an active police investigation. No one comes in or out without the chief's approval, and I'm certainly not going to let you waltz in and take whatever you'd like. I don't even have any way of knowing that what you want is actually yours. If you have proof, you can petition the court to get your property back after the case is resolved."

"It wasn't that kind of deal," Bonner explained as he reluctantly backed off.

"Then I'm sorry, but it sounds as though you're out of luck."

"You didn't even get him to *sign* anything?" I asked the pawnbroker incredulously. How could he run a successful business that way based on a handshake in this day and age?

"Like I said, I've been floating him for years. I never thought he'd stiff me in a million years."

"But it turns out that he's the one who got stiffed," I said with a frown.

"I don't care. One way or another, I'm getting my stuff back," Bonner said softly.

It wasn't soft enough, though. "What is it you supposedly own that was in Mr. Willis's possession?" the officer asked.

"A very expensive orange ring," I filled him for him. "The victim bought lots of orange things from Smiley here over the years."

Smiley was definitely not living up to his nickname as he glared at me.

"The chief was wondering about that shrine of his. She wants to know what's missing," the cop explained. "Maybe you should stay right here while I call her."

"There's no need to involve your boss," the pawnbroker said plaintively.

"We'll let her decide that," the cop said. "In the meantime, you all need to stay right where you are."

"Oh, trust us. We're not going anywhere," Grace explained.

I'd had some dealings with Chief Liddy Holmes, the chief of police of Maple Hollow, in the past, and I wished that I could say that they'd all been good, but that would be stretching the truth quite a bit.

The second she showed up and got out of her squad car, she headed straight to us. "You two again? I thought I told you both to stay out of my town a long time ago."

"We're fine, thank you for asking. How are you, Chief Holmes?" I asked her as sweetly as I could manage given the circumstances. It wouldn't do to alienate her any further than we already had in the past, especially if we had any hopes of getting her help, which was doubtful at best.

"Truth be told, not great. I've got a murder to solve." She turned to her officer. "What's going on, Pickering? Have these two been giving you trouble?"

The young officer looked confused. "Not them. Him," she said as she pointed to Bonner.

"Calvin Bonner. What have you done this time?" the chief asked him.

"I'm just trying to get my ring back," the pawnbroker complained sullenly.

"I assume you have paperwork on it?" the chief asked him.

"Maybe," he answered evasively.

"Maybe?" she asked. Did he honestly think she was going to let that answer slide?

"I have proof enough that it's mine," he said. "Unless you can find a bill of sale, which there isn't any, I'm claiming it."

"That's not my concern, but if it's in there, it's not leaving anytime soon."

"What do you mean, *if* it's in there? Isn't it still in his display?" the pawnbroker asked her.

"It's not apparent, but several things appear to be missing," the chief told him. "You wouldn't happen to know what Willis had in his collection, do you?"

"I saw it a few nights ago," he admitted, "but I don't see how that's going to help me get my ring back."

"Help us, and maybe we can help you," she said. "Maybe."

"Why not? I mean really. What other choice do I have?" Smiley answered glumly.

"That's the spirit." They started inside, but when Chief Holmes saw that we were following them, she stopped and turned to us. "Where do you think you two are going?"

"They knew Willis, too," Smiley said, giving us an unexpected voice of support. "What could it hurt putting a few more pair of eyes on his stuff?"

The chief wanted to say no—I could see it in her expression—but her curiosity as to whether we could help got the better of her. I for one wasn't about to admit that I had no idea the kinds of things Willis collected, but I wanted to see that display, and a quick glance over at Grace showed me that she felt the same way.

"Fine, but nobody, and I mean nobody, touches anything. Understood?"

"Yes, ma'am," Grace and I said in complete sync, while Smiley just shrugged.

"Fine. Let's get this over with. I can't make any money if my store's closed."

We walked into Mitchell Willis's house, and I was immediately overwhelmed with the color orange. From the shag carpet to the lampshades to the furniture, it was an orange nightmare, though he clearly must have thought it was a paradise.

The chief took it in, too. "I'm surprised the walls aren't orange."

"He tried that once," Smiley said, "but everything just blended in, so he painted them white again." Proving that he had been there before, Smiley headed back to what most folks would call the den or the parlor, but in this case, it was a shrine to the color orange. Two traffic cones marked the opening, and I spotted the orange hazmat suit on a dummy in one corner. There were several other pieces along the sides of the room, but the real stars were mounted on the long wall. Occupying two dozen shelves of various shapes and sizes, Willis's collection was clearly the work of one man's obsession. Everything from orange salt and pepper shakers to orange soda bottles—untapped—to vintage Troll dolls sporting bright-orange hair lined the wall.

There were only three spots that were empty, but it clearly hadn't been by design.

I'd leaned forward to confirm my guess when I felt the chief's hand on my shoulder. "That's close enough, Suzanne."

"There's a bit of dust outlining the items that were taken," I pointed out. "You can see the shape of them by the impressions."

She nodded. "I caught that, too. I've already had them photographed."

Whether she had or not was not up for debate, and I certainly wasn't about to call her on it. I wanted to take my own set of pictures, but I had a feeling that would just get us thrown out.

"The ring was right here," Smiley said sadly as he pointed to one of the empty spots.

I could see a solid round line in the dust. "It was on a stand."

"Yeah, he wanted to show it off," Smiley said. "He even put a spotlight on three of his things."

"The three things that are missing," Grace added.

"So, one was his ring," the chief said.

"*My* ring," Smiley corrected her.

"*A* ring," she modified. "It was orange, I take it?"

"The stone was an orange diamond," Smiley said.

"What was it worth?" she asked.

"I was going to sell it to Willis for fifty grand if he could come up with the money in time."

"So, you just loaned it to him in the meantime?" the police chief asked skeptically.

"I've done it before with him, and it's always worked out in the past. Once he has...had something in his hot little hands, he'd move heaven and earth to find a way to pay me for it."

I didn't doubt it, seeing what we were seeing. As I scanned the remaining display items, I noticed something. "The porcelain figurine with the jeweled belly button is missing, too."

If nothing else, it gave me credence in claiming that I had met Mitchell Willis before today.

"You're right, it's gone," Smiley said.

"There's one more item that's missing," the chief noted.

"I have no idea what was there," I said, pointing to the third open spot, telling the truth, for once.

Grace shook her head. "I don't know, either."

"Beats me," Smiley said, "but I'm guessing it was worth a pretty penny."

"Thank you for your cooperation," the chief said. "You may all leave now."

"That's it? That's all I get for cooperating?" Smiley asked.

"If the ring turns up and no one else claims it, we can talk," she said.

"Yeah, fat chance of that ever happening," Smiley snapped. "I'm out of here."

After he left, I started looking around Willis's home. He must have fed most of his money into his obsession, because he lived in rather spartan conditions otherwise.

"I said we're finished here," the chief told us, and Grace and I knew that we couldn't push her any more.

"I just want to stop off at the bathroom on the way out," Grace said as she moved toward the bedroom.

"Find a gas station," Chief Holmes said, blocking her way.

"Fine. A girl can ask, can't she?" Grace asked with a smile.

"She can, but she can't always get what she wants," the chief answered.

"But sometimes she gets what she needs," I intoned.

"I'm not going to stand here and play song lyrics with you two. I have a murder to solve."

I wasn't about to add anything to that, but in my mind, I silently said, "So do we, Chief."

Before we left, I said, "I didn't realize the murder happened in Maple Hollow," knowing full well that it had taken place in Union Square.

"It didn't," she said abruptly as she showed us out, practically shoving us out the front door as she spoke. "But when one of my people gets murdered, I *make* it my business."

"I get that," I said.

As we were starting to leave, the chief said, "Tell your husband I said hello."

I nodded. "Will do," though I wasn't entirely sure when I would convey her message. Jake was an attractive man, especially to women in law enforcement, and while I trusted my husband completely, I wasn't so sure about the women who were attracted to him.

Even happily married women get jealous sometimes.

And men, too, if past performance was any indication.

Chapter 8

"WHERE TO NOW?" GRACE asked me as we got back into my Jeep.

"I'd like to see where they found the body," I said. "Do you feel like a trip to Union Square?"

"That sounds good to me," she said.

"It just occurred to me that we don't know exactly *where* Willis's body was found in Union Square," I said.

"I'll find out," Grace said as she pulled out her cell phone.

"Do I need to even ask who you're calling?" I asked as I glanced over at her.

"Can't a wife check in with her husband at the end of the day to see how he's doing?" Grace asked me with a wicked grin.

"She can, but we both know that's not why you're calling him," I answered as I snuck a quick peek in her direction.

"I can do more than one thing at a time, Suzanne. I'm a great multitasker," Grace said as her husband answered. I kind of hoped she'd put it on speaker, but alas, that wish went unfulfilled.

After a minute of back-and-forth conversation, she hung up. "We need to go to the alley between Sixteenth and Seventh Streets when we get into town."

"That's where the body was found?" I asked.

"According to my unnamed source, it is," she replied.

"Unnamed? Really?"

"Suzanne, we have to play these games sometimes. You know who it was as well as I do. I refuse to directly relate the name of my source to you, so if anyone asks, you can honestly say that you don't know how we found out where the health inspector was murdered."

"Okay, unnamed it is," I said.

"Chief Erskine, do you have a second?" I asked the relatively new police chief for Union Square after we walked over to the taped-off crime scene, marked off with bright yellow-and-black tape.

"No, not really," he said brusquely before he even realized who we were.

"Okay. That's fine. I'll come back in an hour with Jake Bishop, my husband. Maybe you'll have time for him."

"Or my husband, Chief of Police Stephen Grant," Grace piped in as we both took out our cell phones in unison.

"Hang on, ladies," the chief said quickly. "There's no need for that. I thought you were reporters when I saw you approaching."

"I'm insulted," Grace said with mock severity as she looked at me. "How about you?"

"Lumping me in with the likes of Ray Blake and friends is a bit of a slam, isn't it?"

"I wasn't talking about Ray Blake. I said *reporters*," the chief added with the hint of a smile.

"That's more like it. I knew there was a reason I liked you," I told him.

"I like you both too, but there's not much I can give you about the murder. I'm still trying to figure out what happened."

"I thought he was hit in the face with a frying pan," I told him.

"It was a large flat object clearly swung with a great deal of force, but I don't know yet if it was a frying pan or not until I can find the murder weapon," the chief said, parsing his words carefully.

"I just thought it was accepted as fact that was what the killer used, given the range of suspects you must be looking at," I said.

He shrugged. "I'm trying not to take anything for granted," he admitted. "But yeah, it was probably a frying pan."

"I wonder if it was orange," Grace said lightly.

"Orange? Why would it be orange?" Chief Erskine asked her.

"Didn't you know?" I asked. "The late Mr. Willis had a penchant for collecting all things orange, including expensive jewelry."

"How did you manage to uncover that already?" he asked.

"You should call Chief Holmes in Maple Hollow," I said. I really wanted to pump the man for more information, but it appeared, at least for the moment, that Grace and I had a better handle on this case than he did. Maybe it was the fact that three local police chiefs and their respective areas of jurisdiction were all involved. That would make it tough to coordinate everything and keep everyone current on the ongoing investigations.

"I guess that makes sense. Willis was from Maple Hollow," Chief Erskine said with a nod. He glanced back at the taped-off area. "I wish I could let you check it out, but this is as close as you're going to get. Sorry."

"No worries, Chief," I said. There really wasn't much to see anyway. The alley had clearly already been covered, and anything remotely of interest had been removed, since there wasn't a rubbish bin, trash can, or dumpster in sight.

"If you ladies will excuse me, I need to make that call," he said as he stepped away.

Once Chief Erskine was out of earshot, Grace asked, "Did we have to give him that much information at the *beginning* of our conversation?"

"The truth is that I felt bad holding out on him," I replied honestly. "After all, he's just trying to do his job in a bad situation."

"I can see that," Grace conceded. "Where does that leave us, though?"

I looked around the alley and then realized where we were. "Grace, which would you say was closer, Napoli's or Twenty-First Southern?"

She thought about it a moment before answering. "I'd say we were halfway between the two restaurants if I had to guess. Why? I don't get it."

"That's the point. I don't, either," I answered. "We know that he went from Twenty-First Southern to Napoli's, so why would he backtrack and come this way?"

"Maybe he ran into someone outside of Napoli's after he had that argument with Sophia," I said.

"And he headed back this way to get away from them?" she asked me.

"That, or whoever it was forced him into this alley so they could kill him without any witnesses," I answered.

"Either way, it still looks bad for Sophia and Barton," she said. "Which one should we speak with first?"

The prospect of going back to Napoli's after what had happened earlier wasn't all that appealing to me even after Angelica's apology, but neither was confronting the arrogant and surly chef. Finally, I decided to go with Barton Gleason. After all, maybe I could get something else loose from him if I pushed the man a little bit harder. If he bit me for asking, I'd just have to bite right back. "Let's go talk to Barton again and see if we can get a little more information from him. He wasn't exactly bubbling over with information before, but that may have been because Emma and Sharon were close by."

"Do you think he's hiding something from them?" Grace asked as we started walking toward the new restaurant.

"I think it's possible," I admitted, though I hoped that I was wrong.

If Barton did turn out to be the killer, it would devastate Emma, and not just romantically. She and her mother were all in on the restaurant being a success, and that would be hard to accomplish without the amazing chef that everyone coveted.

The front door to Twenty-First Southern was still unlocked, which kind of surprised me. Did they just leave it open for whoever might wander in? I was about to call out that we were there when I heard a woman's voice.

It wasn't Emma or Sharon, but I still recognized it.

I put a hand on Grace's shoulder and put a finger to my lips.

"I don't understand," I heard the woman say.

"It's complicated," Barton answered.

"It shouldn't be, though," she insisted. "I'm just asking you to tell the truth."

Barton was about to answer when Grace must have brushed against a table, sending a water glass that had been sitting on the edge crashing to the floor.

"Who's out there?" Barton snapped as he appeared from the kitchen, brandishing his weapon of choice, the large, flat-bladed meat cleaver. "Suzanne? Grace? What are you two doing creeping around in my restaurant?"

"It's Emma and Sharon's place, too," I reminded him. "We came to talk to you. Hello, Antonia," I said to the DeAngelis daughter standing in the shadows behind Barton.

"I was just leaving," she said hurriedly, beginning to blush. "Thank you for the recipe, Chef," she said to Barton as she raced past us out the door.

"What was that all about?" I asked him pointedly. What had we just interrupted? Had he been cheating, or about to cheat, on my friend, Emma?

"It was restaurant business," he answered angrily. "I'm not going to talk about Mitchell Willis, so if that's why you're here, you wasted a trip."

"That doesn't sound like someone with nothing to hide to me," Grace told him.

"No? Well, it sounds like someone who's getting ready to open a new restaurant. I don't have time for foolishness right now."

"Or monkey business, either?" Grace asked brazenly.

"You don't know what you're talking about," Barton said, the edge growing harder in his voice with every word. "Good-bye."

"Funny, but I thought you'd want to clear your name of murder," I told him.

"I didn't do it. I know it, and that's all that matters to me," he said with a frown.

"Your *partners* don't agree with you," I told him. "Do you even know how much Emma and Sharon have riding on this?"

"They invested their inheritance. It was a good investment," he said as though it pained him to have to justify it to us, mere mortals. Usually, Barton was pretty levelheaded and easy to get along with, but the pressure he was under was clearly showing the cracks in his normally placid façade.

"They've done more than that. Sharon has mortgaged her future, too," I said. Okay, strictly, it wasn't my place to tell him that, but if he was even thinking about bailing on the women, either emotionally or otherwise, he needed to be set straight.

"You don't know what you're talking about," he said, clearly surprised by the news. "How could you possibly know that?"

"Maybe because I listen," I told him. "Barton, what was Antonia really doing here?"

"You heard her," Barton said abruptly. "She wanted a recipe."

"Is that *all* she wanted?" Grace asked him.

"This conversation is over," Barton said, swinging the cleaver in the air and hitting the dull side into his palm. "Good-bye."

"We'll be back later," I told him.

"Whatever," he snapped as we left.

"Was that what it looked like?" Grace asked me once we were out on the sidewalk in front of the restaurant.

"I'd like to think it was as innocent as Barton made it out to be," I told her.

"Sure, and I'd like to believe in the Tooth Fairy and that a nickel candy bar still exists too, but I doubt either one is true," she said.

"Maybe nothing's happened yet," I said.

"Suzanne, you are many things, but naïve isn't one of them. I just have one question for you. Why aren't you calling Emma and telling her what we just saw?"

"It's kind of awkward without any proof, don't you think?" I asked her.

"Let me put it this way. If I'd found Jake having that conversation with one of the DeAngelis girls, I couldn't dial your number fast enough. Tell me you wouldn't do the same thing for me if that had been Stephen and not Barton in there."

"You're right," I said as I pulled out my phone. "As hard as it's going to be, it still needs to be done."

"Good girl," Grace said.

I called Emma's number, hoping that she wouldn't pick up so I could leave her a lame voicemail instead of talking to her directly.

No such luck.

"Hey, Suzanne. What's up? Don't tell me that you found the killer already."

"No, not yet," I admitted. "We just left Twenty-First Southern, and Barton was less than cooperative."

Emma sighed. "He's in full-on chef mode, isn't he? I don't know what to do with him! He's driving us both crazy. Mom and I will speak with him. He'll be better the next time you talk to him. I promise. Is that all?"

I wanted to say yes with all my heart, but I knew that Grace was right. I couldn't let my friend down like that, even if it could very well cause her a great amount of heartache and pain. "No, it's not."

After too long a pause, she prompted me. "Go on. You can tell me anything."

"Barton wasn't alone when we got to the restaurant," I said, winding up to tell her what we'd found and how Antonia had reacted to our sudden presence.

Oddly enough though, Emma beat me to it. "Was Antonia there again?"

"As a matter of fact, she was," I admitted. "Why don't you sound surprised?"

"He told me last night that she's been after him for months, but he won't give in."

"And you believe him?" I asked her.

She actually laughed. "Trust me, he's not giving that recipe to anyone. She can bat those long lashes all she wants, but Barton's white sauce recipe is sacrosanct with him. To be honest with you, I'm surprised she's still trying to get it from him."

"And that's *all* there is to it? Are you sure?" I asked, not wanting to pursue it but not able to let my employee and one of my best friends just dangle like that.

"You mean you thinks that she wants *more* than his recipe? I don't believe it," she said simply.

"Okay, then," I replied.

"You don't sound convinced, but you don't have to be," Emma said somberly. "He shouldn't have blown you off, though. Like I said, I'll talk to him. Thanks for calling. Bye."

Before I could protest any further, she hung up on me.

"Well, that didn't go as I expected it to," I told Grace, sharing Emma's response. "Could she be right? Could it have been a simple misunderstanding on our part?"

"I guess," Grace said with a shrug.

"But you don't think so, do you?"

"The truth is that neither do you, but there's nothing we can do about it. You told her what we saw, or at least you tried to. It's not on your head now. She's a big girl, Suzanne."

"That doesn't mean that I don't still want to protect my friend," I said.

"Just be there for her if and when it all falls apart," Grace answered. "That's really all that friends can do."

"Okay, but if he's cheating on her or even thinking about it, no meat cleaver is going to keep me from scalping him on the spot," I told her.

"Be careful what you say in public," Grace said as she looked around to see if anyone might be listening to us. "You know better than most not to make threats in public. They have a way of biting back later."

"If something happens to Barton because he's been fooling around behind Emma's back, then I *should* be on the list of suspects, no matter what I say in public or otherwise." I'd warned Angelica not to threaten anyone in public, and now I was doing the same thing. I couldn't help myself, though. He needed to be taught a lesson, one way or the other, and I was just the gal to do it.

"Gotcha. I understand. Message received. Don't cross Suzanne Hart."

"Or her friends, including you," I said. "Now, let's go see if we can talk to the DeAngelis clan about what happened earlier."

"Are you talking about the murder or Antonia's behavior?" Grace asked as we headed off on foot toward Napoli's.

"Yes to both," I answered, wondering how many ways I could cross the DeAngelis clan today and live to tell about it.

Chapter 9

ANTONIA WASN'T AT THE restaurant when we got there, though, so at least that part of the awkward conversation couldn't happen until later. Thank goodness for small favors.

"Suzanne, thank you for coming back," Angelica said as Grace and I walked into the kitchen of the Italian restaurant.

"Of course," I said as I looked around. "Where's Sophia?"

"I sent her home," Angelica said. "She was in no shape to work this evening."

"I really need to speak with her," I said, doing my best not to be too aggressive when it came to the woman's youngest daughter.

"I'll have her come back in," Angelica said.

"We could always run by your place and speak with her there," I offered.

"No, she'll need to be here to talk to you."

"Angelica, you trust me with her, don't you?" I asked her, looking deep into her eyes. "You know I'm on Sophia's side, don't you?"

"I do," Angelica said, frowning as she stared down at her hands. "I'm sorry again. Go on, go talk to her. I don't need to worry about you. I know that."

"Get her back here," Grace said, surprising us both by stepping in.

"Excuse me?" Angelica asked her.

Grace said softly, "We all know that you're going to worry, no matter what you say. Wouldn't it be better if you were with her, to support her if she needs you? She went through a pretty traumatic experience. The girl could need her mother by her side."

"You wouldn't take offense if I did that, Suzanne?" Angelica asked me.

"Grace is right," I said, knowing that it was true. "I'm not trying to pull anything over on either you or Sophia. It would probably be better for all concerned if we speak with her here."

"I'll call her right now," Angelica said as she pulled out her phone.

Ten seconds later, the restaurateur put her phone away. "That's odd. She didn't pick up."

"Maybe she's taking a nap or she's in the shower or something," I offered.

"Unlikely," Angelica said as she dialed another number and put this one on speaker. It was answered immediately.

"Antonia, it's your mother. I'm here with Suzanne and Grace..."

Before she could finish, the woman's daughter started babbling. "Nothing happened, Mom! I didn't *do* anything! I *wouldn't* do anything! You have to believe me!"

Angelica looked confused by the outburst, to say the least. "What are you talking about, child? I'm looking for Sophia."

"She took a walk," Antonia said quickly. "She told me she was leaving her phone here so she could be alone with her thoughts."

Antonia tried to hang up, but her mother was too quick for her. "Don't you dare go anywhere, young lady. What have you been up to?"

"Me? *Nothing.* I told you that," Antonia protested.

"Find your sister and bring her to the restaurant. Now!" Angelica replied. It was clear from her tone of voice that she wasn't making a request; she was issuing an order.

"Now, what was that all about?" Angelica asked as soon as she got off the phone.

"It's none of our business," I said.

"I'm asking you to tell me the truth," she insisted.

"Are you serious?" Grace asked her incredulously. "Angelica, your track record at the moment isn't all that great with either one of us as far as our relationships go. If we tell you what we saw, you're probably just going to throw us out, and while I wouldn't mind it nearly so much, I think if it happened twice in one day, Suzanne would never recover."

I wasn't sure I liked Grace stepping in like that, but then again, maybe she'd just done me a huge favor by not making me say it myself.

"That's fair enough, I suppose," Angelica said after a few moments of silent contemplation. "Very well. I'll find out from Antonia herself soon enough."

I couldn't take *not* telling her though, not having the guts to share some potentially bad news with a friend. After all, hadn't I just done the same thing for Emma?

"Angelica," I said after taking a deep breath. "We found Antonia and Barton at his restaurant, having a conversation that, on the face of it, could have been bad, and when she knew that we were there, she couldn't get out of the place fast enough. We don't know anything for sure, but it certainly looked bad."

Angelica frowned, started to speak, and then she clearly changed her mind. After another moment, she nodded. "Thank you for sharing with me. Maria told me that Antonia was spending far too much time there with Barton, but I dismissed it out of hand. Perhaps I rushed to accept her explanation too quickly."

Antonia burst into the kitchen and immediately shot a look of anger toward Grace and me before turning to her mother. "I don't know what they told you, but it's not true," Antonia burst out.

"The truth is that they wouldn't tell me anything," Angelica said. "Your guilty conscience betrayed you, not these two women. You owe them both an apology."

"For what? I didn't say a word to them," Antonia protested.

"For the angry looks you gave them," her mother said. "They didn't deserve that, neither one of them."

"I'm sorry," Antonia said in turn to each of us. "I just thought…"

"Did you, really? *Did* you think? About *anything*?" Angelica asked her softly. "Is there a reason for me to be disappointed in you, child?"

Antonia looked down at her hands, and then to my surprise, she burst out crying. "I was just...it was all so harmless. Everyone flirts. It just...got out of hand...we didn't even kiss. I just felt so...guilty," she said through the tears. "I told Barton he had to tell Emma that we'd been flirting, but he refused. He said it was all in my head, but I know that wasn't true. I'm so sorry, Mom. Please don't hate me."

Angelica took her daughter into her arms and held her until the tears stopped. "I could never hate you, but I've warned you before. There's no such thing as innocent flirting. You are an extremely beautiful woman, and I know how good it feels to get a man's full attention, but you must be more careful, Antonia. It's not fair to anyone involved."

"Hey, let's not forget that Barton has to take some of the blame too," I said. "Antonia can't help how she looks."

"Looks? No. Acts? Yes. I'm not concerned with Barton Gleason at the moment, though," Angelica said.

"You don't have to worry about me, Mom. I'm *through* with men," Antonia said firmly.

"No one's asking that of you," her mother said. "Just make sure they are available before you bat those eyelashes at someone new."

"I can do that," Antonia said as Sophia walked into the kitchen.

"What's going on? What did I miss?" the youngest sibling asked.

"Nothing," Angelica and Antonia said simultaneously, as though they'd rehearsed it.

"Why don't I believe either one of you?" Sophia asked as she looked around the kitchen again. This time, there was clearly some fear mixed with dread in her expression. "Why did I have to come back so soon?"

"We need to talk about what happened earlier," I told her. "But if you aren't up to it, we can do it later."

I glanced at Angelica, who nodded her approval in my direction.

Sophia took a deep breath, looked around again, and then squared up her shoulders. "No, now is as good a time as any. Let's get this over with so I can get back to cooking."

"Sophia, I told you, after this, you can take the night off," Angelica reminded her.

"I know, and believe me, I appreciate it, but there's nowhere else I'd rather be than right here. Is that okay?"

"Of course it is," Angelica said as she wrapped another daughter in her embrace. After a moment, she pulled away. "I'm proud of you, little one."

"Thanks. I'm really something special, wouldn't you say?" she asked with a hint of her usual wicked grin. It appeared that the old Sophia—the brash, self-confident, sassy one—was trying her best to come back.

"I would," her mother agreed.

"Okay, then. Ladies, let's get this over with," Sophia said as she turned to us.

"I know this isn't fun," I told her, "but it's necessary."

"If you say so. I'm not sure what else I can tell you, though," Sophia answered.

"Take a moment and think back to earlier today," I said. "Don't rush it. Go over everything that Mitchell Willis said to you."

"It won't be hard to do. The conversation is kind of burned in my brain," she answered.

"You never gave me specifics earlier," I reminded her. "As closely as you can, tell me what was said."

"Okay," she said, taking a deep breath. Angelica was nearby, but so far, she hadn't intervened. I wasn't sure I could count on that being true the entire time Grace and I were there, but I'd take whatever I could get.

"Whenever you're ready," Grace prompted her.

"He said, 'Hello, little lady. I'm sorry to say that your restaurant didn't pass inspection today. You're going to need to do some work before I can allow you to serve customers.'"

"How did you react to that?" I asked her.

"I was in shock. Mom makes sure we run a tight kitchen. You could *eat* off the floors. I wouldn't personally, but they are really that clean."

"So what did you say?"

"I told him to get stuffed," she said a bit abashedly.

I tried to suppress a smile. "I'm sure he just loved that."

"Not so much," Sophia replied. "He took a step too close to me and said, 'You might think this is a laughing matter, but if you don't pay me $5,000 by tomorrow morning, I'm shutting you down. It's not so funny anymore, is it, little girl?' He grabbed my arm, and that's when I hit him, but only to get him off me! It all kind of freaked me out. I popped him in the chest once with my free hand, and that was it."

"What happened next?" I asked her when the information wasn't forthcoming. "Did he fall or anything like it?"

"No, but he backed into that shelf and knocked some things over," she said as she pointed to a nearby shelf holding the flour and a few other things.

"Did it hurt him?" Grace asked softly.

"Just his pride," Sophia replied. "I tried to apologize, but then he told me that I could forget his offer to help us get a good rating and that tomorrow morning, bright and early, he was going to shut us down, no matter what."

"That must have been tough to hear," I said gently.

"I told him to get out and that if he tried anything like that, I'd tell my mother," Sophia said as she glanced obliquely at Angelica. "Sorry about that, Mom, but you can be the scariest person I know."

"When it comes to my girls, my restaurant, and my friends, I take that as a compliment," Angelica replied proudly.

"Good, because that was how I meant it," she said.

"What did Willis have to say to that?" I asked.

"After he took a second to compose himself, he said that on second thought, he was tired of dealing with the kitchen help and that he'd be back later to talk to the real person in charge," she answered.

"He was talking about me, no doubt, but why he thought I'd react any differently than Sophia did is beyond me," Angelica replied.

"Do you have any idea where he was going next?" I asked Sophia. From where his body had been found, I knew that he'd been on his way back to Twenty-First Southern, but I wanted to know just how much Sophia knew.

"I assumed that he was going to hit the next restaurant on his list, but on his way out, his phone rang."

"Did you hear who it was on the other end?" I asked her.

"No, but somebody must have said something to make him angry, because he was even snippier with them than he'd just been with me."

"What did he say to this mystery caller?" Grace asked.

"That's the thing. It was one of the shortest conversations I'd ever heard. Once he knew who it was, the only thing he said was 'Don't go anywhere. I got held up, but I'm on my way.' As he was putting his phone away, he must not have realized that I'd followed him out the door, because when he saw me standing there, he was clearly furious that I'd eavesdropped on his conversation, for what little good it did me."

"What happened then?"

"I panicked," Sophia admitted, "and I jumped back into the kitchen, and then I dead-bolted the lock behind me. If he was going to come back to say something else to me, he was going to have to come in through the restaurant. I was ready for him, just in case, but he never came back. I know I had a rolling pin in my hand when you came in, Suzanne, but I never hit him with it. I didn't hit him with anything. One little shove with one hand, that was all. Suzanne, Grace, you've got to believe me. He was alive when he left here this afternoon."

"We believe you," I told her as Grace nodded as well.

Sophia surprised us by hugging us each in turn. "Thank you. It's important to me that you two don't think I killed that man, no matter how icky he was."

"It's going to be okay, Sophia," I told her, and after a few seconds, she released me.

"I hope so. I don't know how I'm going to ever sleep again knowing that a killer is out there somewhere on the loose."

"Don't you worry, child. Suzanne and Grace will figure this out," Angelica said, "and they'll do it quickly, too."

I just wished I had her confidence in us, but there was nothing else for us to say.

As we were leaving, I told Sophia, "If you think of anything else, no matter how simple or even unrelated to this, call me, okay?"

"I will, but that's all I know." She turned back to her mother and added, "I'd like to get back to work now, if that's okay with you."

"Of course it is," Angelica said with a warm smile for her youngest daughter.

The matriarch nodded to me as Grace and I left. I knew that it was meant to be reassuring, but it felt as though it was a reminder that we were on the clock now, in more ways than one. A lot was riding on us figuring out who had killed the health inspector, and soon.

I just hoped that Grace and I were up to the task.

Chapter 10

I WAS ABOUT TO SAY something to Grace when my cell phone rang.

It was Emma Blake. Had she reconsidered her thoughts about Barton and Antonia? I had new information on that score, but whether it would ease her mind or not I really couldn't say.

"Hey," I said after I told Grace who was calling.

"Suzanne, you need to go to Twenty-First Southern," Emma told me.

"And get stonewalled again by your boyfriend? I don't think so," I told her.

"He'll cooperate this time. Trust me," Emma said sternly. "Mom and I had a little chat with him, and he's seen the error of his ways."

I highly doubted that was even possible, given the current state of things. "Which errors are those, exactly?" I asked, wondering if they'd discussed more than Barton's lack of cooperation with our investigation.

"I told you, there's nothing to what you saw earlier," she answered, dismissing the subject firmly. "Now, do you still think he might be able to help, or not?"

"We're on our way," I told her. "We're just leaving Napoli's, so it won't take us five minutes to walk back over there."

"How is...everyone there?" Emma asked nonchalantly. At least, that was how it would probably sound to someone who didn't know her as well as I did. I had a feeling that Emma knew that something was up, and I got the impression that she wasn't sure herself whether she wanted to pursue it or not despite what she'd told me earlier. Hinting around about it wasn't going to work with me, though. She'd shut me down, and if she wanted to know what I knew, she was going to have to ask me a direct question. Only then would I feel good about sharing what I'd overheard at Napoli's.

"They're coping," I said. "Sophia's getting some of her spirit back, which is a very good thing, and the rest of the ladies are rallying around her."

"Good. That's good," Emma said, letting her voice trail off a bit as she spoke.

"Well, we're almost there," I told Emma, lying outright, since we hadn't moved much during our brief conversation. "Talk to you later."

"Don't be gentle with him, Suzanne," Emma instructed me. "It's okay to bust his chops about dismissing you two earlier."

"Thanks. I'll keep that in mind," I said as I hung up before Emma could give me any more instructions on how to handle this case.

"What was that all about?" Grace asked as we actually started moving toward the soon-to-be-opened restaurant.

"Emma told us that she and Sharon had a chat with Barton. Supposedly he'll be more cooperative this time."

"Well, in their defense, he could hardly be *less* cooperative than he was earlier," Grace said. "How did Emma sound to you?"

"Like she wants to believe everything is peachy keen, but she just can't bring herself to do it. She told us we should take the kid gloves off when we spoke with Barton."

Grace shook her head and laughed a bit. "Is that because of his earlier refusal to talk to us or her suspicions that he's up to something?"

"Your guess is as good as mine, but I'm thinking that it's a little bit of both."

"So, are we going to take her advice and go after him?" Grace asked me, clearly relishing the opportunity to put the chef in his place about his behavior with us, the DeAngelis daughter, and more importantly, Emma and Sharon.

"Let's see how it goes," I said.

When we got to the restaurant, Barton wasn't in the kitchen, which surprised me given how soon the place was about to hold its soft opening.

Instead, he was sitting at a table with his hand on his chin, clearly pondering something. Something was obviously troubling him. Could it have been murder?

"Barton, are you all right?" I asked as we walked inside.

"What? Yeah, I'm fine."

"Maybe you are, or it could be that Emma is close to being finished with you and your behavior," Grace told him, letting the statement snap a bit as she delivered it.

To be fair, she hadn't agreed when I'd said that I was going to see how things went before I verbally smacked Barton around a bit. Clearly, she had decided to jump right in.

"I don't see how this is any of your business," he said defiantly as he stood.

"Emma *is* our business," I said before Grace could agree with him.

The young chef shook his head as though he were trying to dismiss us with a gesture. "So I've been flirting with Antonia. What's the big deal? Did it get a bit out of hand? Maybe, but how is that my fault? I do that, you know? It's my way of dealing with people. I thought it was all harmless enough, but then Antonia said she felt guilty about our interactions and insisted that I tell Emma all about it. I have no intention of doing that."

"Did things go further with you two than just talking?" I asked him.

He just shrugged in reply, making me wonder.

"Emma deserves to be treated better than that, and you know it," Grace snapped. "So if you can't focus on her, you need to let her know so she can move on." I knew that Grace had been cheated on a time or two, but hey, I'd lost a husband to an affair, so if anyone had the right to be sensitive about the subject, it was me.

"Nothing has to change," he said.

"Do you want someone's advice who has been there?" I asked him.

"I've got a feeling I'm going to get it whether I want it or not, so go ahead."

I bit my lower lip, and then I said, "Straighten up and get your head out of the mud! I tried to tell her what we saw earlier, but she wouldn't let me. She obviously doesn't want to know, and if all you've done is chat Antonia up, then stop it right now and start paying more attention to Emma!"

I glanced over at Grace and saw that she was stunned by advice. "Straighten up? Really? Is that the answer you're going with, Suzanne? Did you feel that way when Max cheated on *you*?"

"That's just it. Max *cheated* on me. Barton's just been flirting with Antonia, and who knows how many other women. Is it fair to Emma or Antonia or even the rest of them? No, but you can't compare his behavior to what my husband did to me. Now can we *please* drop this and discuss Mitchell Willis?"

"I promised I would talk to you. Tell me what you want to know," he said reluctantly.

"Tell us more about your encounter with Mitchell Willis," I told him.

"I already told you everything that happened. It wasn't pretty, and I'm not particularly proud about the way I behaved, but I didn't kill the man. I just killed his cell phone." Again with that smirk, no matter how serious the situation was.

"Are you honestly trying to be *cute*? You can save your so-called charm, because it's not going to work on us," Grace told him with an edge to her voice, clearly not able to get over his earlier behavior.

"I'm telling you both the truth whether you believe me or not," he said, keeping his answer brief and to the point.

"So, you have nothing new for us?" I asked him, staring hard at the chef to see if I could tell whether he was lying to us or not.

"Nothing."

"Then we're wasting our time here," I said.

As we turned to go, Barton said, "There was one thing, but I don't think it's all that important."

"Tell us anyway," I told him.

"As Willis was storming out, my fresh produce supplier came in through the back, and he nearly tripped over his own feet when he saw her, he was so enchanted. Trust me, Simone is nice and all, but she doesn't merit that kind of reaction on her best day."

"Really?" I asked, and then I had a hunch. "Simone's a redhead, isn't she?"

"How could you possibly know that?" he asked me. "Does she supply you, too?"

"No," I answered.

"It is true, though, isn't it?" Grace asked.

"As a matter of fact, that's the best thing she's got going for her," Barton answered. "Her red hair is beautiful, curly, and nearly down to her waist. Otherwise, she's a bit of a plain Jane. Why? Did Willis have a thing for redheads?"

"Orange things, to be exact," I said, and a new train of thought came into my head. Was there any chance his boss, the woman he'd been infatuated with once upon a time, was a redhead? It might be worth checking out, especially if she dyed her hair and he lost interest in her when she started dating *her* boss.

There was one thing you could say about Mitchell Willis.

He was consistent.

Grace and I were making our way back to my Jeep when I saw something in the street, catching the light. I'd been looking down the road as a street sweeper approached us, and I'd been surprised to see it there. The shard was leaning against the street curb three hundred feet from the restaurant—between a jewelry store and a real estate office—a shining piece of something that looked out of place. Ordinarily,

I would have walked right past it, but something made me stoop over and look at the fragment a bit closer.

When I did, I felt a chill go through me.

The moment I got a better look at it, I could tell that it was clearly part of a porcelain figurine, the bottom legs and part of the skirt broken off the main body.

Though I'd never seen the statuette myself, I had to wonder if this might be a part of the missing belly dancer from Mitchell Willis's collection.

But the question remained: where was the rest of it? And had it been robbed of its jewel, the most valuable part of the piece?

Without a word to Grace, I wrapped the shard in my handkerchief and handed it to her.

"Check this out," I said.

"What's this?" she asked me.

"Unless I miss my guess, it's part of Mitchell Willis's belly dancer," I said as I hunted around for any other pieces or, more importantly, the jewel itself, since it was by far the most valuable part of the piece. "We need to be quick before that street sweeper gets rid of the evidence."

"Over here," Grace called out a few seconds later once she knew what we were looking for.

"Did you find the jewel?" I asked her.

"No, but unless I miss my guess, this is the rest of the statuette," she said as she added the other found pieces to mine.

"We need to call Chief Erskine right now," I said as I pulled out my phone and stepped out of the way of the sweeper, which was barreling down on us at two miles an hour but was relentless like the tide.

"Couldn't we do that *after* we talk to Barton about finding this?" Grace asked me.

"I'd like to, but I'm not sure it will do us much good. Maybe the chief will have more luck with him than we have."

"Is Chief Erskine going to be upset we removed evidence?" Grace asked me.

"I don't see how he could be. If we hadn't grabbed it all up, there wouldn't have been anything to find," I said.

"Chief Erskine, this is Suzanne Hart," I said once I got him on the line.

"Suzanne, I'm sorry, but there's really nothing more I can tell you about the case. It's an ongoing investigation," he said.

"I'm not looking for information, I'm providing it," I told him.

Or at least I thought I had. When there was no response, I glanced at my cell phone and saw that the man had hung up on me before I'd even had the chance to speak again.

"Okay, it looks as though it's time for Plan B," I told Grace grimly. "Chief Erskine just hung up on me. Let's go see what Barton has to say about this," I added as I held out my hand for the pieces of the broken statuette we'd collected.

"What's that?" Barton asked as I held the shards of the statuette out to him. "Did you drop something on your way in? I hate to say it, but I don't think there's enough Super Glue in the world to fix that thing."

"Are you saying you don't recognize what it was?" I asked him sharply.

He took another look at the pieces and then shook his head. "No, should I? It looks like some kind of woman, but I don't have any idea where it came from."

"We do, though," Grace told him. "It was one of Mitchell Willis's prize possessions."

"You don't happen to know what happened to the gemstone that was in the woman's belly button, do you?" I asked him.

"If I didn't recognize the statuette, how would I know anything about the stone?" he asked me, getting a little salty in his reply.

"Clearly, we're wasting our time here," I told Grace.

"Hang on," Barton said. "Was that gem valuable?"

"It was," I said, based on what Smiley had told us. It had been nearly in the center of Mitchell Willis's display, next to a ring that was worth close to fifty thousand dollars. He'd told us that the statuette had been worth six grand, but most of that had to have been from the gemstone. "Listen, it doesn't look good for you. Once the chiefs of police hear about us finding these shards so close to your restaurant, you're going to be in for a great deal more heat than just us hounding you. If you have anything to tell us, and I mean anything, now is the time. Maybe we can help you, but not if you don't tell us the truth." I hoped that my words rang true with him. I'd used the line before on a suspect but never someone so close to me.

"I'd tell you if I could, but I can't. What do you want me to do, *lie* to you?" he asked.

"It wouldn't be the first time, would it?" Grace asked, piling on a bit more.

"Get off my back, Grace," he snapped, finally tired of my friend's prodding. "Napoli's isn't that far from here," he added, clearly scrambling for anything that would take the focus of our investigation off of him. "How do you know someone there didn't do this?"

As if on cue, Angelica DeAngelis stormed into the restaurant, glaring at Barton without giving either one of us a second glance.

"Angelica, what are you doing here?" I asked, though it was obvious that she was out for blood.

"Suzanne, I say this with as much love and respect as I can have for you, but this is about Antonia and nothing else."

"I get that," I said as I took a step back to get out of the line of fire.

"Leave my daughter, all of my daughters, alone. Do you understand me?" Angelica asked as she got within two inches of Barton Gleason's nose.

"Nothing happened, Angelica," Barton tried to explain, but she wasn't in any mood to listen to it.

"It's *Ms.* DeAngelis to you from now on, *Mr.* Gleason," she said, making his last name sound as though it were an insult.

"I don't know what to tell you," he said simply. "It won't happen again."

"You're right, it won't. But if it does, if you cast so much as a lingering glance in the direction of *any* of my daughters, there will be consequences."

"Angelica, you can't threaten him in front of witnesses, no matter how justified you might be," I reminded her, thinking about how I'd done the exact same thing earlier. Barton's behavior was causing him to be threatened more than I thought possible, and if something happened to the young chef, there would certainly be a host of suspects, with my name again at the top of the list. "If something happens to him now, we'll have to tell the police what you said."

My friend looked at me and smiled with a grin that belied the anger clearly seething just below the surface. "Suzanne, you and Grace both have my blessing to run to the authorities if something happens to Mr. Gleason here, because odds will be good that I *did* have something to do with it."

Without another word, she turned on her heel and walked out of the restaurant.

Barton started after her, but I put a hand on his arm. "Don't."

"But I just want to..."

"Just don't," I said. "Trust me."

Grace added, "Listen to her, Barton. She's trying to help you, no matter how little you might deserve it at the moment."

The chef paused a moment or two, and then he shrugged. "Fine. That's all I need, the owner of the best restaurant in town hating me. What else could go wrong?"

"You could be as dead as Mitchell Willis is," Grace said and then quickly glanced at me. "For the record, that wasn't a threat, Suzanne. I was just pointing out to him that things could almost always get worse than they already are."

"I agree," I told her. "Don't forget though, being arrested and tried for the man's murder wouldn't improve matters much for him, either."

"That's fair," Grace said.

"On what world is any of this *fair*?" Barton complained.

"The world we live in isn't always fair, but it's the only one we've got," I answered. "Now, for the last time, did anything else happen when Mitchell Willis was here earlier?"

"Nothing," Barton said, but I could swear there was a hint of hesitation in his words.

"We don't believe you," I said, speaking for Grace but knowing that even if she hadn't heard that hitch in his answer, she'd back me up.

After all, that was what we did.

"I can't do anything about that though, can I?" Barton asked after pondering his answer for ten full seconds.

Without another word, Grace and I followed Angelica's lead and walked out of the restaurant without even a single glance back at the arrogant chef.

Chapter 11

"WOW, I SINCERELY HOPE nothing happens to Barton in the next few days," Grace said as we made our way back to my Jeep.

"That's funny, I didn't know you cared," I said with a grin after we got in, buckled up, and started heading back to April Springs.

"You know as well as I do that I don't want to have to rat Angelica out to the police. The truth is that I'm not Barton's biggest fan at the moment."

"I caught that earlier, but then again, I'm more perceptive than most," I answered with another slight smile.

"Okay, I admit I've been a little hard on him, but you were right. He was lying to us just then."

"By *not* telling us what was on his mind," I said.

"That's one of our three favorite ways to lie, isn't it?" she asked.

I nodded as I said, "You can lie outright, or you don't tell *everything* you know, or you tell the truth so badly that people are convinced you're lying, even when you're not. That last one is the hardest one to pull off, but it's also the most convincing."

"That sounds about right to me," she said.

"Something else is going on with you though, isn't it?" I asked her as I drove back to April Springs with our newly found evidence.

"I don't know what you're talking about, Suzanne."

"Really? You're going to try that with me? Denial? Why are you being so hard on Barton? I know you and Emma are friendly, but you're not *that* close. He's being a real jerk, but if she can put up with it, why can't you?"

We rode in silence for ten minutes, which usually wouldn't be a problem, but for us, given the awkwardness of it, it was a lot to take. I was determined not to say another word until Grace did, though.

Finally, she spoke. "Stephen's been flirting some lately too, and I guess I might be a bit overly sensitive about it at the moment."

"Has he been targeting anyone in particular, or is it just a change in his general behavior?" I asked her softly.

"Oh, it's someone in particular all right," she admitted.

"Care to share a name with me?" I asked after a few more moments of silence.

"Dr. Zoey Hicks," she said.

"Got it," I answered. I knew the young doctor/coroner could act a bit too over the top at times, dressing suggestively and cooing a bit too much in the presence of any man who paid her the slightest bit of attention. She'd even been caught flirting with our police chief in the past, but I'd thought that foolishness was behind us. "What exactly did you see? Did Stephen do something?"

"It's not so much what my husband does when she's around, it's the way he acts," Grace said. "You know, when I say it out loud, it sounds crazy even to me."

"Crazy hasn't stopped either one of us in the past," I reminded her. "Have you told Stephen how it makes you feel when he acts that way?"

"Sort of," Grace said. "Okay, not really. Not at all, truth be told. As a matter of fact, I don't want to give him any ideas in case this is all just in my imagination."

"If it helps, the young doctor flirts with my husband, too," I told her.

"She flirts with everything in pants," Grace said. "How do you handle it?"

"I don't worry about her all that much," I admitted. "I know my husband. Nothing is ever going to happen, so I don't spend a whole lot of time thinking about it."

"You have a great deal of faith in him, don't you?" Grace asked me.

"And you should have just as much faith in Stephen," I told her. "He truly loves you, and you know it."

"I hate to even say it, but you had faith in Max once upon a time too, and that didn't turn out all that well," Grace said softly.

"True, but I knew that Max could *never* love me the way our husbands love us," I told her. "If it would help, we can both pay a little visit to Dr. Zoey Hicks's office and put the fear of two fierce April Springs women into her heart."

That made Grace smile, which was saying something given the circumstances. "Let's put that on the back burner and solve this case first, shall we?"

"We can surely try," I told her.

After another few minutes, Grace asked me, "So where do we go from here?"

"Honestly, I was just sick of all things Union Square, so I made an executive decision and decided to head back to April Springs."

"That sounds perfect to me," she said.

"There's really only one thing left for us to do at this point anyway. If we can't get Chief Erskine to look at the broken figurine we found, we need to at least find *someone* in law enforcement who will listen to us."

"Are you thinking we should share what we found with Stephen when we get back?" she asked me.

"If he'll give us more time than Erskine did," I said.

"He's my husband, remember? He'll give us the time, or he's going to have a great many more problems than he realizes," she answered with an expression that I knew all too well. I doubted Stephen Grant had been that stupid a day in his life to ignore his wife, especially if he'd seen the look I was seeing.

"Then let's give it a shot," I said.

As we neared the end of our drive back home, Grace asked, "What do we do after we turn these remnants over to Stephen?"

"To be honest with you, I haven't thought that far ahead," I admitted.

"I want you to *always* be honest with me, even if it makes you look foolish, reckless, or even feckless," she said with a grin.

"Right back at you, toots," I said.

"Toots? Really?"

"Yeah, it sounded bad even as I said it. I know what you told Stephen. No nicknames, right?"

Grace shrugged. "That's what I said, but if you really want to open that door, be my guest. Just remember, I can give at least as good as I get."

I couldn't imagine the number of nicknames my best friend might give me even on the spur of the moment, but one thing was certain: I didn't want to find out.

"Sorry. Please forgive me. It's Grace. Just Grace. Always Grace from here on out," I said with a slight smile.

"I thought so," she replied, and then we both started laughing.

It might have seemed odd in the middle of a murder investigation, but we'd both needed a little fun and frivolity given the circumstances.

The laughter was short-lived though, as we soon returned to April Springs and went in search of the chief of police, who also happened to be Grace's husband.

"Stephen, Suzanne and I need to see you," Grace told her husband after calling him and putting the conversation on speaker as we were coming into the April Springs city limits.

"Grace, things are kind of crazy right now. Could we maybe..." he tried to say before she cut him off.

"No, we can't maybe anything. This is important," Grace said firmly.

"I'll meet you in my office in five minutes," Stephen said, clearly picking up on the cues from his wife.

"I love you. You know that, right?" Grace asked him.

"Of course I do. I love you, too. See you soon."

"He sounded baffled by that last bit," I said with a grin.

"Let him wonder. It's good for him," she answered, smiling back. "You were right. Thanks for talking me down off the ledge."

"Does this mean you'll back off Barton a little bit from here on out?"

"A little bit? I can probably manage that," she answered.

I had to laugh. "You are one tough broad. You know that, don't you?"

"I might be, but I can only dream about being as tough as you are," she replied.

"Seriously? You're crazy," I said.

"I thought we'd already established that," Grace answered as I pulled into the police station behind city hall.

"Let's go," I said as I parked and got out of my Jeep. I was heading for the door of the station when I heard someone calling out to us.

"Over here, ladies," the chief said. That was when I noticed that he wasn't alone.

Jake was there, too.

"Are you two boys playing nice?" I asked them.

"Suzanne, we're both a long way from being boys," my husband said, but I noticed the hint of a smile on his lips as he said it.

"Don't try to kid a kidder," I told him.

"What's so important?" Chief Grant asked us. "Not that it's not a pleasure seeing you both, but Grace, you made it sound as though you had something you needed to talk about."

"We found something in Union Square we need to show you," I said as I dug the shards out of the bag I'd stashed them in back in town.

Chief Grant backed up when I tried to hand it to him. "If you found something there, you should have called Chief Erskine."

"We tried," Grace said, clearly getting frustrated by the situation. "He wouldn't even hear us out. Don't tell me you're going to do the same thing. What do we have to do, drive to Maple Hollow and give this to Chief Holmes? Doesn't *anyone* want to solve this case?"

Her words stung him a bit, that much was clear by his reaction to her scolding. "I'm sorry. I should have known you two would have tried to do that first. What have you got?"

"I'm not sure he deserves to see what we found, Suzanne," Grace said to me, pretending to turn away from her husband.

"Give him a break, Grace. It can't be an easy situation for him to be in, trying to coordinate efforts across three separate jurisdictions," I told her.

"Okay, that's fair," she said. "Go on, then. Give it to him."

"What exactly is it we're getting?" Jake asked as he watched me hand the police chief the evidence we'd discovered.

"Unless we miss our guess, it's the belly dancer statuette that was stolen from Mitchell Willis's shrine to all things orange," I answered.

"Hang on. We don't know for a fact that it was stolen," the chief said.

"Okay, missing. Can we at least agree that it was missing?" I asked him.

"Yes, that I can do." He put on a pair of gloves taken from his back pocket and pulled out the shards we'd found. "It's broken."

"Don't blame us," Grace said quickly. "It was like that when we found it."

"And you called Chief Erskine, but he wouldn't retrieve this himself?" Chief Grant asked us.

"He wouldn't even hear us out," I said.

"What's this about a street sweeper?" Jake asked.

"It was thirty yards away from obliterating the evidence when we saw these pieces lying on the street by the curb. As it was, there may be a few pieces missing, but that's the most we could find on such short notice. Take it and be grateful."

"We are," Chief Grant said. "We need to dust these pieces for fingerprints." He paused a moment before asking, "Where exactly did you find these?"

"On the road between Twenty-First Southern and Napoli's," I said. While it was strictly true, it had clearly been closer to Twenty-First Southern, but I didn't want to put a noose around Barton Gleason's neck if I didn't have to.

"I don't suppose you were able to get pictures of exactly where you found these before you retrieved them," Jake said.

"We could have gotten you photographs or the shards themselves but not both," I told him. "I feel as though we made the right choice."

"Of course you did," Jake said. "That was good police work, ladies."

"Thank you," Grace and I said in nearly perfect unison. "What are you going to do after you dust these for prints?"

"We'll call the respective chiefs and let them know," Chief Grant said. "You didn't happen to find the jewel in the belly, did you?"

"No, if it was there, we didn't see it. Maybe the street sweeper got it. You should ask the Department of Sanitation or whoever is in charge of those things," I said. "Why? Do you know anything more about the piece than you did before?"

"Just that the gemstone was really the only valuable part of the piece," he said.

"Smiley told us that, too. Sorry, we should have mentioned that," I said.

Jake and Stephen let that slide. "We had a long chat with the man, probably the least friendly pawnbroker I've ever met in my life, and he finally came clean with us. Smiley Bonner does not like officers of the law in any way, shape, or form."

"Did he happen to confess to killing Mitchell Willis?" I asked.

"No such luck, but he finally told us that the stone in the belly dancer's navel was valued at close to twenty thousand dollars," the chief replied with a flash of a wry smile.

"That creep lied to us!" Grace protested. "He claimed that the entire piece wasn't worth over six grand."

"He was probably trying to pick it up for a fraction of its value," I said.

"The man wouldn't know the truth if it came up and bit him on the nose," Grace said.

"I don't disagree with that," Stephen said with a shrug. "But it doesn't make him a killer."

"No, but I doubt he'll be winning any Ethical Businesspersons of the Year awards, either," I answered. "So, where does that leave us?"

"Us? So, it's *us* now?" the chief asked.

"Well, I figure bringing you those shards was worth something," I said.

"Honestly, if I had anything to share, I would," the chief said. "So far, we're not making much progress. I was kind of hoping the other chiefs were having more luck than we were."

"Unless I miss my guess, they're having even less now that you've got one of the missing items back in your possession," I said. "I can't believe someone was brazen enough to kill the health inspector in broad daylight, even if it was in an alley that's not that well traveled."

"The thing is, it could have been," Jake said. "That tells me this wasn't some carefully planned-out assassination. It was clearly a crime of passion, but then, we already figured as much."

"Were you working on the assumption that Willis's murder didn't have anything to do with the rash of extortion attempts he's been making lately?" I asked, clearly surprised by the idea.

"We haven't ruled anything out yet," the chief said. "The killer may have found out about the extortions and then decided to take advantage of them by using them as cover for his or her own motives for killing him."

"Wow, that never even occurred to me," I told them honestly.

"That's why we're the professional crime solvers," Jake said with a smile. "Seriously though, you two did good work."

"Thank you, sir," I told him.

Stephen spoke up, clearly a bit embarrassed by what he was about to ask. "Grace, do you have a second?"

"I've got all of the time in the world for you, big boy," she said with a smile.

"Big boy?" he asked, clearly baffled by the new nickname.

"Hey, you tried it with 'kiddo' for me, so Suzanne and I were thinking about trying out nicknames for everybody we know," she said, lying through her teeth.

"Let's make that a hard pass, okay?" the chief asked.

"That's fine by me," she said, and then she glanced over at me. "I don't want to say I told you so, but I told you so."

"What can I say? You were right, and I was wrong," I admitted, going along with her harmless fib.

"That's what I love from you when we disagree, Suzanne, absolute and complete capitulation," Grace replied.

"Way to be gracious about winning," I told her as I stuck my tongue out at her.

"Of course," Grace answered as her husband touched her arm.

"A moment, please?" He reminded her of his request.

"We'll be right back," Grace said as she and the chief stepped away for a little bit of privacy.

"What's that all about?" Jake asked me as we watched them having an earnest conversation.

"Do you *really* want to know? It's most likely about their domestic harmony, or disharmony, as the case may be," I told him.

Jake shook his head. "You're right. I figure it's 'need to know,' and I don't need to know. How are you doing with all of this? Have you seen Angelica again?"

"We're all good; well, mostly," I told him. "I just hope I don't let her down, or Emma or Sharon, either. They're putting a lot of pressure on me to solve this case, and quickly."

"At least you're not the only ones working on it," he said.

"Thank goodness for that. Between all of us, hopefully, we'll be able to crack this murder sooner rather than later."

"Suzanne, is that a good sign or a bad one?" Jake asked as he pointed to Grace and Stephen. They were hugging tightly, and it appeared that Grace was crying. "Are those happy tears or sad ones?"

"Do you honestly think I can tell that all the way from over here?" I asked him.

"I kind of did," he admitted. "Sorry."

I studied Grace's body language, and after a moment, I said, "They are happy tears. Definitely happy tears."

"You're some kind of odd, woman," he told me with a grin as he wrapped me up in his arms. "It suits my kind of odd perfectly though, so we're good."

Ordinarily, I wouldn't have stood for anyone calling me odd, but coming from Jake, somehow, it was a compliment. "Right back at you, my main man."

"I thought we'd decided not to do nicknames," Jake said with a frown.

"Just teasing," I told him and kissed him to show it was true.

"All right. Break it up, you two. We've got a murder to solve," Grace said, smiling as she wiped the last tears from her cheeks.

"Yes, ma'am. We're on it," Jake told her as he and the chief headed inside.

"See you tonight," Chief Grant told his wife with the hint of a smile.

"Not if I see you first," Grace answered, laughing a bit, which made his smile grow even that much more.

I was so glad they'd found each other. They were an excellent fit. But I was even happier that I'd found Jake. It had taken kissing a few frogs to finally find my prince, but it had been worth the trouble.

"Everything good?" I asked her once we were alone again.

"Not yet, but we're getting there," she said with a nod.

"That sounds fine to me. Now, let's get cracking. I want to take another stab at Smiley and see what else he might have held back from us."

"That could be fun," Grace said. "I'm going to enjoy interrogating him."

"I pity him that, but then again, he brought it on himself," I told her as we got back into my Jeep and headed back to Maple Hollow. It was a shame no one was paying me for the miles I was driving. If we didn't solve this case soon, I was going to have to dip into my meager savings for gas money.

Chapter 12

WE GOT TO SMILEY'S and parked on the street near his entrance. I didn't want him to know we were coming so he could prepare himself. We had the element of surprise at the moment, and I aimed to keep it as long as we could.

The only thing was, though, the surprise ended up being on us.

We were four steps from the front door of the pawnshop when we were nearly run over by Gert Leister, the information desk receptionist at the county government offices.

What was more, she was stuffing a wad of cash into her oversized metallic purse when she bumped into us.

"Hello, Gert," I said merrily. "That looks like a load of money."

"What? No, it's nothing. Really," she said, clutching the massive purse to her chest. "And it's Ms. Leister, not Gert," she added lamely.

"Gert," Grace said, ignoring her request of honorifics. "You must have pawned something nice to get that much money out of Smiley. What did you just get rid of?"

"That's none of your business," she snapped, getting her assurance back. "Now if you'll excuse me, I need to get home. It's getting late."

"That sounds good. We'll see you first thing in the morning at work. I'll call your boss tonight and set up an appointment for all four of us so we can talk about what you've been up to lately," I bluffed. "I'm sure he'll want to know."

"You know *Mr. Wimple?*" she asked me, her face suddenly going ashen.

"My husband is a former state police investigator," I told her. It was the truth, even though it had no bearing whatsoever on what I'd just threatened.

"So?" she asked, going a bit rigid.

"He *knows* people," Grace added with a smug look. That was true as well. Hey, we had just found a fourth way to lie: stating facts that had no relevance to the matter at hand and making it seem as though they did. I'd have to write that one down.

"Listen, you've got it all wrong. I didn't do anything I shouldn't have. So what if Mitchell Willis gave me an orange necklace a month ago to try to get my attention? It wasn't worth much, and since it was mine to sell, why would I want to keep it to remind me of someone who just got murdered?" she asked lamely. "Besides, it wasn't worth much. Smiley only gave me a hundred dollars for it," she protested. "Do me a favor. Please don't tell Mr. Wimple. After the mess of having two supervisors out on leave because of their baby, he doesn't like us fraternizing in any way, shape, or form. He wouldn't understand."

"I won't say anything to him, at least not *this* time," I said after hesitating ten seconds, pretending to chew it over.

"Thank you," she gushed. "I owe you one. Now, I've got to go."

And with that, she left us.

Smiley was still grinning to himself when we walked into the pawnshop. "I'll be right with you," he said as he finished putting a necklace with an orange stone into the display case. I saw that he'd priced it at fifteen hundred dollars, quite a markup compared to what Gert Leister claimed to have gotten for it.

"What can I help you... Oh, it's you two," Smiley said, his grin fading away. Was that why they called him Smiley, because he grinned whenever he cheated someone else? The nickname fit much more than his overall disposition did.

"Wow, that's quite a markup you've got on that necklace," I said as I looked at it through the glass.

"I'm entitled to make a fair profit," he explained.

"Fifteen hundred percent, though? Do you really call that fair?" I asked.

"Hey, I don't *force* anyone to take the deals I offer," he said with a wave of his hand.

"It's just too bad," Grace said as she stared at the necklace.

"For my customers?" he asked. "Such is life."

"No, I was talking about you," she said as she pulled out her cell phone.

"Don't try to bluff me, Grace," Smiley said. "I'm much better at it than you'll ever be."

"I know," Grace said. "That's why I'm not bluffing." She waited a moment before dialing. "Is there anything more you want to tell us about Mitchell Willis before I make this call?"

"No," he said flatly.

"Okay, but remember, you had your chance." She hit a few buttons on her phone, and then she said, "Chief Grant, this is Grace. We just saw Gert Leister from the county government offices leaving Smiley's pawnshop. She pawned a necklace she claimed Mitchell Willis gave her for a hundred dollars. Smiley has it for sale already priced at fifteen hundred, but I'm thinking it might be evidence. Okay. Sure, we'll wait here and make sure he doesn't try to get rid of it."

Smiley laughed when Grace put her phone away. "That was well done. I have to give you credit for doubling down. Now, how long are you going to stick around until you realize your bluff isn't going to work on me?"

A few moments later, the front door opened, and Maple Hollow's police chief walked in instead of Stephen Grant.

"Where's this necklace?" she asked Smiley as she approached the counter.

"It's not evidence of anything!" Smiley snapped. "I bought it fair and square."

"Use gloves and hand it over," she said, ignoring his protest.

"But I bought it," he protested.

"If it was stolen, you just admitted to receiving stolen goods," the chief said.

"I didn't know where she got it," he yelped. "She said that it was a gift."

"It's orange, and she had a relationship with the deceased. Are you telling me you didn't figure that part of it out all on your own?" Chief Holmes still hadn't even glanced at us, but I was fine with that. After all, we had front-row seats for the show.

"I didn't ask her where she got it, and she didn't say," Smiley admitted.

"Hand it over, Smiley," she snapped as she held out an evidence bag.

"Fine, but I want a receipt," he snarled.

"Oh, I'll write you one the second it's in my possession," she answered.

He finally did as she'd instructed, and after she sealed the evidence bag, she wrote him a receipt and handed it over to him. "Have you taken anything else of value in today that happens to be orange, by any chance?"

"No, ma'am," he said with a frown.

I had a hunch. "How about during this past week?"

The chief wasn't happy about me butting in, but she could see that she'd limited her question a bit too much. What if someone had stolen something from Willis earlier, and he'd discovered the theft and accused whoever took it? That could certainly lead to murder in a back alley.

"No, nothing," Smiley snapped. "Look around if you don't believe me."

"That won't be necessary," Chief Holmes said. "Thank you for your cooperation."

"I'm going to want my property back," he reminded her.

"Which piece are you talking about now?" Grace asked him with a sweet feigned smile.

"*All* of it," Smiley said.

"Well, at least he already paid you for the figurine that was missing," the chief said, watching him closely as she said it.

"The belly dancer? He didn't get that from me. What about her? Has she turned up?" he asked. "I'd be interested in buying that piece once this was all over. I'll give the police a good price, fair market value."

"Sort of. Do you mean the six thousand you told us it was worth or the twenty grand you told our husbands it was valued at?" Grace asked him.

Smiley's face fell, but it soured even more when Chief Holmes added, "Sorry, but at this point, it doesn't really matter, since it's been destroyed."

Smiley looked genuinely upset by this information. "Is that really true?"

"We found it ourselves," I admitted.

"But not the gemstone that was worth so much," the chief said. "When they found the pieces of what was left of it, the stone was gone."

"I thought you said you found it?" he asked Grace and me.

"We found *pieces* of it," I admitted, "but whoever took it must have known that the stone was the only truly valuable part of it. Someone like you," I added.

"Hey, I didn't take anything, and I surely didn't kill Mitchell," he protested. "Now, unless you want to take something else that belongs to me, I'd like you all to leave."

"Thanks again for your cooperation, Smiley," Chief Holmes said as she bounced the evidence bag in the air.

"Sure," he said bitterly. "Always happy to cooperate."

Once we were outside and nearing my Jeep, I assumed Chief Holmes would go on her way, but she surprised me by following us instead.

"Thanks for coming on such short notice," Grace told her. "I'm glad Stephen could get ahold of you so quickly."

"Chief Grant asked me, so I came," she said. "Thanks for the tip."

"Are you going to talk to Gert Leister about the necklace?" I asked her.

"Right after I leave here, but I wanted to talk to the two of you first."

Oh, boy. I had a hunch we were in for another lecture. "Honestly, we were just trying to help," I said, trying to get in an explanation before she could start scolding us.

"And I appreciate that," the chief said, surprising me by actually smiling at us. "I'm beginning to think that I've misjudged the two of you. It appears that you can add some value to my investigations after all."

"Thanks?" I asked, as much of a question as a statement.

"You're welcome," she said as she handed us each a card. "If you find anything else out about the case, and I mean anything, call me, day or night. I put my home phone number on the back, along with my personal cell phone number. I'd like to be your first call."

"My first call will always be to my husband," Grace told her. I felt like adding that I'd be doing the same thing, but it felt a bit redundant to me.

She nodded. "I get that, and if you find something in April Springs, by all means call him first. But if you stumble across something in my town, I'd like to be the first person to hear about it. This cooperation is fine and all, but Maple Hollow is my responsibility, and I feel as though I lost one of my own today."

She made a good point pleading her case, which surprised me in a way. It was by far the nicest Chief Holmes had ever been to us, that was certain.

"We'll make sure you're informed," I said, not committing us to agreeing to her terms one way or the other.

I could see that she wanted to push for a more definitive answer, but I could also see that she knew she wasn't going to get it. "That's all I'm asking," she said as she started toward her squad car.

On a whim, I called out, "Is there any chance we can tag along for your interview with Gert Leister?"

"Sorry, but I'm afraid that she won't tell me anything if civilians are there. You understand, I'm sure."

"Of course," I said with a soft smile that showed I wasn't all that surprised by her response.

"What was that all about?" Grace asked once we were in my Jeep heading toward April Springs again. "Was it me, or did she seem a little too eager to be first in line for new information?"

"It wasn't just you," I said. "The question is, why?"

"I don't quite buy the idea that she's taking care of her town, but what other stake could she have in knowing something before Stephen or Chief Erskine?" Grace asked.

"You don't suppose.... No, it's ridiculous," I said.

"Tell me what's on your mind, Suzanne. Remember, it's okay for us to look foolish in front of each other."

"What if *she* had something to do with Mitchell Willis's murder?" I asked her.

"Wow, that's a leap, even for you," Grace said.

"Think about it. We know from personal experience how little the police chiefs are paid around here," I said. "What if she decided to help herself to some of Willis's treasures, and he caught her at it? If he told anyone what she'd done, she'd be ruined."

"Let's say that's true," Grace said, always willing to play along with my hypotheticals. "If that's what happened, why dump the body in Union Square? If she kept it here, it would be much easier for her to muddy up the investigation and steer it away from herself."

"That's a point, but what if she was more afraid of it happening so close to home than she was of transporting the body? By staging it this way, she could put the suspicion on people who had a reason to want to see Mitchell Willis dead and gone far away from her home base," I said.

"I don't know. It seems like a stretch," Grace said after a few moments of thought.

"I know it doesn't happen very often, but we've seen bad cops before," I reminded her. "When I first met Jake, we were dealing with a bad cop, remember?"

"I'm not about to forget Officer Moore," she said.

"Neither am I," I admitted. "I'm not saying Chief Holmes is guilty of anything. All I'm saying is we need to watch our backs around her."

"And everyone else, too," Grace added. "So, what else is new?"

"That's truer than I'd care to admit," I said as I continued our drive back home.

Chapter 13

AFTER DROPPING GRACE off at her place, I drove the small distance up to the cottage, hoping that Jake was back from working with Chief Grant.

His truck was gone, but someone else's car was parked in his spot, someone I didn't really want to talk to at the moment.

That was just too bad, apparently.

"Hi, Emma. I'm sorry, but we just haven't made much progress on the case yet," I told her, trying to stave off her show of disappointment in my lack of skill in pulling off a miracle. I must have made it look too easy in the past, because folks had come to expect me to wave my magic wand and declare the killer almost instantly.

"I'm not here about the murder," she said, and I felt a twinge of relief. "I want to talk to you about Barton."

And just as quickly, that twinge was gone and was replaced by a wave of dread.

"Would you like some tea first?" I offered her. "Or maybe something stronger?" I asked as I unlocked the cottage front door.

"Could we just sit out here and chat?" she asked me, clearly fighting to keep her voice level and unwavering.

"Sure," I said as I took a seat on the porch swing. "We can do that."

I'd half expected her to take one of the chairs, but instead, she sat beside me on the swing. I thought it was a bit close, but then I realized that she didn't want to make eye contact with me while we chatted. Evidently, Emma was expecting a rough conversation, and she was clearly preparing herself for it.

"Where do you want me to start? I'm not sure how much you already know or how much you want to know."

"I have been seeing a side of Barton I haven't liked ever since we started planning to open the restaurant several months ago," she said. "I doubt anything you say is going to surprise me all that much."

"Well, the good news is that he's not cheating on you," I said, and then I added, "At least not that I know of."

"I didn't think he would," Emma admitted. "After all, he's afraid of killing the golden goose where all of the money comes from. When you told me that Mom had mortgaged her future for Twenty-First Southern, I nearly lost it. It was one thing gambling with found money, but things got very real very quickly when I heard that."

"I should have kept my mouth shut about that," I told her.

"No, you did what friends do," Emma reassured me. "I needed to know."

"So, about Barton..." I suggested.

"Suzanne, I know he's a flirt. In a way, he's always been kind of one, but lately, he's been much more brazen about it. He'll even do it in front of me, playing up to all of these women in the restaurant-supply business like I'm not even there. He even told me this morning about a rich older patron who has promised to make big things happen for him and that I could either get on board or get out of his way."

"How does that make you feel?" I asked, immediately regretting sounding like some kind of cheap two-bit therapist on the radio.

"Angry, embarrassed, and basically just tired," she admitted. "The truth is I would have broken up with him a month ago, but we all have too much at stake right now. His treatment of me has been just about unbearable. If I could make it all go away with a snap of my fingers, I would." She paused to get herself under control before she continued.

"I'm so sorry," I told her, patting her hand gently.

She jerked back at the first touch and then apologized. "What did you see, Suzanne?"

"He was having a pretty intense conversation with a woman when Grace and I went back to speak with him," I told her, being as honest as I could.

"Which bimbo was it this time, Antonia or someone else?" Emma asked, shaking her head from side to side.

"I'd rather not say, mostly because she's not a bimbo at all," I told her.

"Really? You're *defending* her?" Emma asked, pulling back a bit from me.

"No, she knows she shouldn't have done what she'd been doing, but she tried to stop it, and she told me that she insisted that Barton tell you about how far their flirtation had gone. It wasn't physical, at least I don't think so, but evidently, it was still pretty intense."

"Okay, so it's a friend of yours," Emma said, letting the words slip out. "I thought *we* were friends, Suzanne."

"We're more than that, Emma," I said, pleading with her to at least hear me out. "We're family. That's why I said something to you earlier. Do you think that was *easy* for me?"

"No, I can see that it wasn't," she said after a moment's reflection. "Who it was really doesn't matter anyway. It's *Barton's* behavior I don't care for. If he wants to be with someone else, he should do that, but I won't have him treating me with so much disrespect anymore."

"I understand that, but what about the money?"

She shrugged. "I'll talk to Mom and see what she thinks. We can still back the restaurant without Barton and I being a couple." Emma stood, as though the decision was enough to get her moving again. "Thank you, Suzanne. I appreciate you being there for me."

"The truth is that I'm not sure I helped at all," I told her in all honesty as I got up from the swing, too. "Do you need to think about this a little more before you talk with Sharon? After all, you and Barton have been dating for quite a while."

"That's never seemed to matter all that much to him, so why should it matter to me?" she asked, fighting back the tears now.

"*You* matter to me," I said as I stepped toward her, wrapping her in my arms. Emma resisted at first, but after a second, she leaned into it and started sobbing for real. I held her, riding out the wave of emotions, for a good three minutes before she stopped.

Pulling away, Emma wiped at her eyes with her sleeve. "Wow, I didn't realize how wound up I was," she said with a slight laugh.

"You have every right to mourn the loss of a relationship," I told her.

"It's funny though; we haven't really been in a relationship for quite a while," Emma admitted. "The money seemed to change everything. He's not the man I fell in love with, that's for sure."

"Is there *nothing* left there that might be salvaged?" I asked her. "I mean, if he stops treating you like dirt and ceases his constant flirting." It sounded ridiculous to me even as I said it.

"Let me ask you a question in return," she said. "Is he a suspect in your mind?"

"I can't rule anyone out just yet," I told her, trying to sidestep the truth.

"That's not what I asked you, and you know it," Emma repeated.

"Yes," I said, "he is very much still a suspect."

I owed her that much, the truth, if nothing more.

"I think he might have done it, too," Emma said softly. "It's crazy, but saying it out loud kind of makes it real, but I feel better than I have in quite a while."

"I'm here for you if you need me, day or night," I said. "You know that, right?"

"I do," she said as she offered me another brief smile just as Jake drove up in his truck.

"That's my cue to leave," Emma said as she took a step off the porch.

"You don't have to go anywhere," I told her as Jake got out and joined us.

"Don't leave on my account," Jake said, and then he noticed that Emma had recently been crying. Sometimes, I wished that my husband wasn't quite as observant as he was, but that came from the years he'd spent as a trained officer of the law, and that was a lot of what made him the man he was. "Emma, are you all right? If someone did something to you, tell me, and I'll take care of them." He said it with the earnestness of a man defending one of his own, and I was as proud of him as I could have been.

"What are you going to do, break Barton's legs?" she asked him playfully.

"If it's called for," Jake agreed.

"No, I'm good, but thanks for the offer. I'll keep it in mind." She even laughed a bit as she got into her car and drove off.

"Am I supposed to know what just happened?" Jake asked me.

I answered by giving him a sweet kiss.

"What was that for? Not that I need a reason," he said with a grin.

"Just for being you," I told him.

"Then by all means, feel free to keep rewarding me for being myself all you'd like," he answered as he swatted my bottom.

"Watch it there, mister," I told him with a smile.

"I will, but you'll have to walk away first."

Evidently, he'd enjoyed his reward, that much was clear.

Changing the subject, I said, "I don't have a thing ready for dinner, and I know you didn't cook. Should we go out?"

"We don't have to," Jake said. "Dot and Phillip have invited us over to their place for ribs."

"Nobody called and asked me," I protested.

"*I'm* the formal invitation," he answered. "I ran into Dot downtown, and she told me Phillip has been smoking way too many ribs on the new smoker he got. She had to run out and get more supplies for the fixings, so she invited us to join them."

"I don't know how I feel about being a last-minute addition to the guest list," I told him.

"Well, I hope you can find something here to eat, because *I'm* not missing ribs for anything."

"Not even me?" I asked him.

"Suzanne, that's not fair. Please don't make me choose between you and smoked ribs."

The poor man looked as though he were about to cry, and I'd had enough tears to last me for at least the rest of the day. "I won't. Let's go."

"That's the woman I fell in love with," he said as he picked me up and twirled me around the porch before releasing me.

"You really do love ribs, don't you?" I asked him.

"Yes, but not as much as I love you."

"It's close though, isn't it?" I asked him with a smile.

"I refuse to answer on the grounds that I may incriminate myself," he responded as he held his truck's passenger door open for me.

I knew some women didn't like things like that, but I wasn't one of them. I liked it when my husband was considerate and treated me specially, especially after witnessing Barton's recent behavior toward Emma.

"Thanks for the invitation," I told Momma sarcastically as we walked into the home she shared with my stepfather.

"Of course," she said, ignoring the sarcasm in my voice. I knew she'd heard it. Since my teen years, my mother had become an expert in my inflections, expressions, and body language of all types. "It was the least we could do."

"Calling Jake was indeed the least you could do," I told her, grinding it in a bit more.

"Suzanne, you're an adult. Act as though that were true, would you?"

"I won't, and you can't make me," I said in a petulant voice.

That got her laughing, and I joined in. My mother and I had our moments of conflict just like everyone else, but at the end of the day, she was one of my best friends, and I didn't care who knew it.

"Where's Phillip?" Jake asked, sniffing the air as though he were expecting it to smell like a restaurant in Lexington, a town in North Carolina famous for its barbeque.

"He's out back, tenting the meat or something. I don't know. The man treats it as though it's some kind of ritual," Momma told him.

"Hey, no blasphemy in my presence," Jake said as he leaned over and kissed her cheek. "I'll be out back if you need me."

"Sampling the fare, no doubt?" Momma asked him.

"I won't ask, but if he offers, I'm not going to say no," Jake replied as he hustled outside.

"He's in a good mood, isn't he?" Momma asked me after my husband left to join hers at the barbeque shrine.

"Most days, he is," I told her.

"Even when there's a murder being investigated?"

"Probably more so then," I told her. "It was what he was born to do."

"I know that. I just didn't realize he was taking part in your investigation," Momma said as she started dishing out coleslaw, baked beans, and cornbread onto platters and into bowls.

"He's not," I told her. "He is, however, helping the trio of police chiefs trying to solve this case together."

"Why isn't he helping *you*?" Momma asked me as I pitched in and started setting places.

"He offered, but I declined," I told her. "Don't worry, Grace is working with me, so I'm not going it alone."

"I should hope not," she said. "So tell me, what progress have you made so far?"

"Do you really want to talk about Mitchell Willis's murder?" I asked her.

"It's the only way I'll be able to hold my own in the conversation after you two leave," Momma explained. "We both know that even as we speak, your husband is telling mine everything he can about the case."

"To be fair, they were both former police chiefs here," I said.

"And we've both taken our turns as amateur sleuths as well," she reminded me. "Albeit one of us had a vastly greater amount of experience than the other."

"Hey, what can I say? I don't go looking for trouble."

"And yet it still finds its way to you with alarming regularity," Momma commented.

"I'd deny it if I could, but I can't, so I won't," I told her. "Do you really want to know?"

"I do," she said.

As we worked getting ready for the meal, I decided it wouldn't hurt telling her about the progress we'd made so far. After all, my mother was a savvy woman, and maybe, just maybe, she'd help clarify the situation in my mind.

Goodness knew I could use it.

"Okay, here's what we know so far, what we think, and who is involved," I started.

Chapter 14

"MITCHELL WILLIS CAME by my shop this morning and threatened to fail me in my health inspection if I didn't 'hire' him as a consultant."

"What! That's criminal," Momma said loudly.

"I know. Listen, this is going to go faster if you save your questions and comments for the end," I told her, and then I added, "Don't worry, I wasn't about to pay him off."

"Good for you," Momma said proudly.

I looked at her and tilted my chin down without saying anything.

She got it immediately. "Okay, *now* I'll be quiet."

I found that hard to believe, but I went ahead anyway. "Jake came by, and we went to the county government offices to talk to his supervisor. Just about everybody there in the chain of command is off on maternity or paternity leave, so we came back to the Boxcar to see if he'd tried to extort money from Trish. He had, so we came up with a scheme to get him back to Donut Hearts so we could gang up on him. Only when I called him, I overheard him fighting with Barton Gleason."

"Emma's fiancé?" she asked, breaking her vow.

"Yes. No. Maybe," I answered, because at that point, any of the three answers could be true.

"You're just doing that to keep me from talking anymore," Momma said with a hint of disapproval in her voice.

"No, that's the truth. I don't know right now. They are having issues. Anyway, I heard Barton and Mitchell Willis argue over the phone, so Jake and I rushed to Union Square to see what was going on. Barton claimed it was nothing, so we went to Napoli's, where we found Sophia, Angelica's youngest, in tears. The man had tried to bully her, and she was taking it badly." I wasn't about to go into being evicted from Napoli's. It really wasn't part of the case, though it was a very important part of my life.

"We couldn't find the health inspector anywhere, so we came back here, where we found out that Willis had been murdered by blunt-force trauma, evidently from being on the wrong end of a frying pan. Emma and Angelica both asked me to dig into what happened, so I called Grace to help out. We found out that Willis was a collector of all things orange, including valuable gems. He owed money to a pawnbroker in Maple Hollow, named Smiley of all things, but he denied killing the man. Chief Holmes from Maple Hollow asked Smiley to look and see if he could tell what was missing from the collection, and Grace and I tagged along as well."

"I've heard that Chief Holmes doesn't put up with foolishness," my mother said approvingly.

"She doesn't," I told her. "Anyway, it turned out that three things were missing, at least as far as we could tell: a ring, a belly dancer with an extremely valuable jewel in her navel, and some mysterious third object. Smiley claimed that the ring, worth fifty thousand dollars, was his, but nobody believes him, though actually, the more I think about it, the more I realize that it could be true. Grace and I went back to Union Square to speak with Barton about the inspector, but he was less than cooperative."

"You'd think he'd want to clear his name," Momma said.

"He might have been terse with us because we caught him with Antonia DeAngelis," I said.

"Poor Emma," Momma said.

"They were just arguing about their flirtation, but it was bad enough. Barton basically threw us out, so we went to Napoli's. Sophia told us that Willis was upset about an appointment he made for later that day with some mysterious caller, and we're still trying to track that lead down. We went back to speak with Barton a third time after Emma called and told us he'd do better, but it wasn't all that great. Barton's gotten some kind of attitude since he started working at opening the restaurant, even though it's Emma and Sharon's money backing him."

"On the way back to the Jeep, kind of halfway between both restaurants, we found shards that were clearly from the belly dancer, but the gemstone was missing, which turned out to be worth over nearly twenty thousand dollars. We went back to Maple Hollow to confront Smiley about it, and while we were there, we saw Gert Leister coming out of the pawn shop with a wad of cash."

"Who is Gert Leister again?" Momma asked.

"Oh, sorry. I forgot to tell you about her. She's the receptionist at the county government offices, and it turns out that Mitchell Willis may or may not have had a crush on her at one time. She claimed that he gave her some jewelry, and she sold it to Smiley as soon as he died. She claimed that Smiley gave her only a hundred dollars, but when we got there, he'd priced it at fifteen hundred. When he wouldn't cooperate with us, Grace called Stephen to tell him about the necklace, which may or may not be evidence, and Stephen called Chief Holmes, who happened to be close by. She took the necklace as evidence just in case, and on the way out, she asked us to call her if we found anything new out. And that's where things stand right now."

"My, you've been busy today," Momma told me. "So, you must have thoughts about what happened to this Willis person. What are they?"

"Momma, it's too soon to even speculate," I told her.

She laughed. "For most people, perhaps, but not for my daughter, the sleuth."

"Amateur sleuth, actually, but really a professional donutmaker," I answered with a slight smile.

"There's nothing amateur about the way you conduct an investigation. Don't hold out on me, Suzanne."

"Okay, here goes. Barton has to be a suspect, and until I can get proof that she didn't do it, so does Sophia."

"I wouldn't tell Angelica that," Momma warned me.

"Do I *look* insane?" I asked her. "I don't think there's a cat whisker's chance that she did it, but she has to stay on the list for now."

"I understand that, but surely you have other suspects."

"I do," I admitted. "There's Smiley Bonner, who I trust about as far as I can throw, then there's Gert Leister and a man named Fred who worked with Willis and knows entirely too much about his collection of orange things, including the value of some of it."

"That certainly sounds like a good place to start," Momma said approvingly. "Is there anyone else on your list?"

"What makes you ask that?" I asked her.

"You're holding out on me, young lady. I can tell by the way you're hesitating."

"It doesn't make sense, but I think there's a possibility Chief Holmes may have had something to do with it," I admitted.

"Why is that?" Momma asked without a hint of disdain or scoffing in her voice.

"She seems awfully keen on getting any news from us firsthand, before we even tell Jake or Stephen. Plus she's had a bit of change of personality, going from wanting to throw us out of town on general principles to looking to be our new best friends. Frankly, I don't trust her," I admitted.

"Trust who?" Jake asked as he walked into the kitchen, followed closely by Phillip with the largest plate of ribs I'd seen outside of Hillbilly's Barbeque a few hours south of us.

"Your truck," Momma said, speaking before I could. She was clearly trying not to upset Jake, but I couldn't let that stand.

"I love your truck, and you know it. The truth is that I don't trust Chief Holmes."

Jake didn't get mad, he didn't explode, he didn't even stiffen. "Why is that?"

"Something inside tells me she's more involved in this than she lets on," I admitted.

Jake nodded. "Trust your gut, Suzanne."

"Do *you* believe it's possible she killed Mitchell Willis?" I asked him, shocked that he hadn't gotten outraged by the very thought that a cop might be bad. "I thought you two were friends."

"We're acquaintances," Jake corrected me. "And I've seen cops go bad before. It's not a pretty sight," he added.

"I had one on my force that was bad once," Phillip reminded me.

"We were talking about him earlier," I admitted.

"Just be careful, Suzanne," Jake said solemnly. "If I were you, I wouldn't share that suspicion with anyone else, even Chief Grant."

"I won't say anything, but Grace is another matter," I told him.

"Why don't you give her a quick call and ask her not to, if she hasn't already? Stephen hasn't been on the job as long as we were." He motioned to Phillip, who clearly liked being included in that comment.

"I'll try," I said, seeing how serious Jake was.

Grace picked up on the second ring. "Hey, long time no see," she answered when she knew that it was me.

"Have you told your husband about our suspicions about Chief Holmes yet?"

"No, and I'm not going to. I don't think we're going to get any rain, but you never can be too careful," Grace replied.

"He's right there, isn't he?" I asked.

"Okay, I'll bring an umbrella tomorrow when we get together after you finish working, but I think you're crazy."

"Thanks," I said.

"See you later, alligator," she replied as she hung up.

"She decided on her own not to tell him," I reported.

"Good. Now that that's cleared up, let's eat," Jake said enthusiastically.

"Are you trying to tell me that you haven't tasted a bite of ribs yet?" I asked.

"I wouldn't dream of lying to you," Jake said. "I didn't have a single bite."

"Did you perhaps have *more* than a single bite?" I asked.

He started laughing, and then Phillip joined in.

"She's good, isn't she?" he asked my husband.

"The best," he said proudly.

After eating way too many ribs as well as fixings, I was stuffed beyond belief.

Then Momma brought out fresh peanut brittle.

"I swear, I'm too stuffed to take another bite of anything," I told her, declining as politely as I could manage.

"Suzanne, try one piece," Momma insisted.

"Dot, if they're too full, don't make them," Phillip insisted.

I got a feeling that I didn't know the whole story here. "Did *you* make this, Phillip?" I asked as I looked at the light-golden pieces of brittle, thin as a whisper and light as a breeze.

"Yeah, but it's not that difficult," he said.

I grabbed a piece and popped it into my mouth. Most brittles I'd had in my life, including my mother's, were hard and crunchy, but this was something else entirely. The candy practically melted in my mouth, and I popped a few more pieces quickly.

"I'll try some of that," Jake offered. He too was impressed. "*You* made that?" Jake asked the retired chief of police.

"Don't act so surprised," Phillip said with a grin. "I made the ribs too, but that didn't seem to surprise you."

"I would think brittle was a lot harder to make than smoking ribs, not that it's particularly easy either," he said.

"It took me all of ten minutes in the microwave," Phillip said proudly.

"I don't believe it," I said.

"Are you calling me a liar, young lady?" my stepfather asked me with a smile.

"No, but I remember Momma poring over a hot stove, making brittle when I was a little girl, and no offense, but it wasn't anywhere near as good as this."

"No offense taken," Momma said proudly. "I agree. Tell them where you learned how to make it, Phillip."

"It was off a YouTube video," he admitted. "I thought it sounded too good to be true, but I figured what did I have to lose? It's pretty good, isn't it?"

"Pretty good? I'd say it's a great deal more than that," Jake said. "I'd like to place an order right here and now for more."

"Today's your lucky day, then," Phillip answered as he pulled out a large Mason jar chock full of brittle. "I made extra, just in case."

"Don't let him kid you. I can't get him to stop making it," Momma said with a laugh. "I'm actually gaining weight being around this man!"

If my mother had gained more than eight ounces in the past ten years, I certainly couldn't tell it. She was always a petite woman with the daintiest of figures, whereas I felt like an extra-large version of her at my very thinnest.

"Hey, what can I say? It turns out that I've got a knack," Phillip said with a grin.

I took Jake's arm and led him to the door. "Let's get out of here before he pushes some chocolate peanut butter balls on us."

"You're safe, at least for now. I'm not making buckeyes until Christmas," he said with a smile, clearly pleased that we'd liked his offerings.

"I'd better lose some weight before then," I said.

"Don't you lose an ounce," Jake said as he squeezed me in his arms. "I love you just the way you are."

"There will be a lot more to love if we keep hanging out here," I told him, pushing him playfully away.

Chapter 15

ON THE WAY HOME, JAKE asked, "What did your mother have to say about the case?"

"What makes you think we talked about murder?" I asked him.

"Suzanne, you are two of the most curious women I've ever met in my life. I refuse to believe that she didn't ask you about Mitchell Willis or that you didn't tell her everything you've discovered and even suspect so far."

"Do you *ever* get tired of being a cop?" I asked him.

"I'm not a law enforcement officer anymore, remember?"

"You may not have a badge, but you'll always be a cop, and we both know it," I told him.

"That's probably true. I noticed you didn't answer my question, though."

"She thought we'd made some progress since we started. After all, we've only been working on it since this afternoon," I told him as we neared our cottage.

"Care to share with me what you told her?" he asked me. "Who's made your list of suspects besides the Maple Hollow Chief of Police?"

"You think we're off-base there, don't you?" I asked him as we parked and headed to the front door. Thank goodness nobody was waiting there to ambush us again. Talking to Emma had taken it out of me, and I wasn't at all sure I could take it if someone else showed up.

"I'm reserving judgment until you bring me something more to back your suspicions up," he said. "Surely she's not the only one on your list."

As we walked in the door, I said, "I don't buy Gert Leister's story that Willis gave away anything orange, but I could be wrong. The man was a collector, not a giver," I said. "I'd love to know how she really got her hands on that piece of jewelry."

"I'd be interested in that myself," Jake said.

"Hey, no fair sharing what I tell you with the other police chiefs," I told him. "This is just between us."

"You never said we were off the record," he answered as he spun the white plastic lid off the jar and grabbed another piece of brittle.

"Don't hog it," I said, reaching for another piece myself. "That's for both of us."

"We'll eat it until it's gone, and then you can find out which YouTube channel Phillip got the recipe off of," he said.

"Or you can," I countered.

"Or I can," he agreed.

"Do I really have to tell you something is off the record?" I asked him. "That's going to severely limit our conversations around here when we're both working on a case separately."

"Of course you don't," Jake reassured me. "I just thought our goal was to catch the killer, not to see who gets there first."

"You're right. I'm wrong."

"Excuse me?" Jake asked, looking at me for a moment.

"You heard me the first time, mister. We share whatever helps catch the murderer," I told him.

"Thanks," he said. "So, who else are you thinking of?"

"Hey, I told you one of mine. Now it's your turn," I said.

"I'm not sure Chief Grant would be happy with that arrangement," he said after a moment's thought.

"Jake Bishop, if you think for one second that Stephen and Grace haven't already compared notes, you're sadly underestimating our friends."

"That's fair enough, and besides, Stephen told me that this might come up," he answered with a bit of a grin.

"So then why go through all of that just now?" I asked.

"Sometimes I like to get you worked up just to watch the world burn," he replied, his grin evolving into a full-blown smile.

"You, sir, like to live dangerously."

"I thought we'd established that long ago," Jake answered.

"That's true. Still, it's your turn."

"Smiley is pretty high on our list at the moment," Jake admitted.

"Do you think he's actually got the jewels and the mystery object that he claims he's looking for and claims is missing?" I asked.

"Don't you?"

"I asked you first," I said.

"It's a possibility. I'm having a hard time believing he loaned the ring to Mitchell Willis and was willing to wait for payment, especially without having any written documentation that it belonged to him."

"It does sound out of character," I admitted.

"So Smiley was on your list, too," Jake said.

"Yes," I answered.

"Okay, I went. Now it's your turn again."

"The man at Bar None we met named Fred something or other," I told him.

"Ballantine," Jake supplied.

"You know about him, too?" I asked, surprised.

"We're talking to him tomorrow morning," Jake admitted.

"Grace and I already interviewed him," I said a bit smugly.

"Why do you think he's a suspect?" Jake asked.

"He seemed to know a great deal about Willis's collection," I told him. "He's the one who told us how valuable that ring was. It just figures that he might have been the one to kill Mitchell Willis in order to liberate his valuable collection and convert it into the currency of his choice."

That caught Jake by surprise. "What currency might that be?"

"Beer," I said with a shrug. "The man's a lush, pure and simple. While we were there, he was getting drunker by the minute. He claimed that it was because he had just lost his best and only friend, but I wasn't completely convinced."

"It could have been that he was trying to numb the pain from killing someone," Jake answered after a moment's thought. "I've seen it do that to people."

Sometimes I forgot that my husband had led a hard and very full life before we'd ever met. I had to wonder if he'd turned to alcohol when he'd lost his family in a car wreck. If he had, who could blame him? "Anyway, that's it for us so far. Do you have anyone to add to the mix?" I asked.

"We're looking at his boss, too," Jake admitted.

"The one who is out on maternity leave?" I asked.

"Mitchell clearly had something on her if he wasn't afraid of being fired for extorting you all," Jake explained. "If he were blackmailing her, she might strike out to stop him from telling anyone what he knew about her."

"But she just had a baby!" I protested.

"All the more reason to protect her new life," Jake said with a shrug. "Didn't she make your list?"

"Honestly, she never even crossed our minds," I admitted.

"Maybe that's a good thing. I like that you try to think the best of people, Suzanne."

"That might make us good people, but we should have put her on our list and her husband as well. After all, he works there too, and he has just as much to protect as she does."

"He's on our list for tomorrow, too," Jake said.

"Maybe Grace and I should speak with them as well," I answered.

"Why don't you let us at least see if they have alibis that aren't limited to each other and their newborn before you do anything," Jake asked me gently.

"We will, on one condition," I said firmly.

"Yes, we'll let you know if they have solid alibis as soon as we find out," my husband answered.

"And Stephen won't be upset with you?" I asked.

"I'm pretty sure he would tell Grace anyway," Jake admitted.

I stifled a yawn and tried not to glance at the clock. I knew my bedtime was close, since it usually came right after dinner. It was one of the downsides of being a donutmaker. I was ready for some sleep when the rest of the world was still wide awake, and I was up long before most of the folks I knew.

"On that note, you need to go get some sleep," Jake said. "Sweet dreams, my love."

"Sweet dreams to you," I said as I kissed him and managed to wrest the brittle from his hand when he loosened his grip.

"Hey, that's not fair. You're not going to eat any in your sleep."

"What if I wake up with a craving though?" I asked him.

"Tell you what. Let's divide up what's left into two equal portions. That way, you can sleep-eat all you want to," Jake answered with a grin. When I didn't deliver the jar back to him, he moved toward me. "Just because I'm smiling doesn't mean that I'm not serious. Hand it over, Suzanne."

I did so, albeit a little reluctantly. Half was better than none, which is what I probably would have woken up to if I'd let him keep the whole jar, but we'd have to learn how to make that stuff for ourselves.

Or maybe not. I had enough treats and temptations in my life without adding any more goodies to the list.

For a change, Jake's phone woke me, not my alarm.

"Who is it?" Jake whispered, trying to save me my precious little sleep. After a few moments, he answered, "I'll be out front in three minutes."

"Who was that?" I asked, rolling over in bed.

"Go back to sleep, Suzanne," he urged me as he got up and quietly got dressed in the near darkness.

"You might as well turn the light on," I told him as I sat up. "I'm awake."

"You have another two hours to sleep," Jake insisted.

"Until you tell me where you're going, I'll never manage to nod off again," I told him.

"That was Chief Holmes. She had a patrol car checking up on Mitchell Willis's place, and they reported seeing lights on inside that weren't on the hour before on their rounds. She investigated, but she'd like our opinion."

"Yours and mine?" I asked as I started to get up to join him.

"Easy there, slugger," Jake said. "I'm talking about Chief Grant and Chief Erskine."

"Oh. Okay. That makes more sense," I said as I settled back into bed. "Be careful, and let me know what happens."

"Later," he said as he leaned over and kissed my forehead before leaving.

I lay there wondering who, and why, someone would break into Mitchell Willis's house in the middle of the night, but I knew that if there was a clue there to be found, Jake would be the one to uncover it. I had ultimate confidence in my husband. Not only had he been a top investigator for the state police, but he'd been in law enforcement his entire adult life in one form or another, even working as a consultant after he officially retired from the force. Was it dangerous? Maybe, but not nearly as bad as other situations he'd faced in his career. I decided that a few hours' more sleep was the only rational thing I could do, and soon enough, that's exactly what I did. Tomorrow, or technically, less than an hour, was another day, and I'd deal with it then.

For the moment, I needed every second of beauty sleep I could get, especially if I was going to try to catch a killer the next day.

Chapter 16

BY THE TIME I WOKE up, I still hadn't heard from Jake. After checking to see that I hadn't missed any messages, I got ready and went to work. I knew my husband would call me when and if he found anything out. It made me curious why someone would break into Mitchell Willis's house after his most valuable possessions were gone, though.

Or were they? Was there something we'd missed in our earlier, admittedly cursory search of the place? Was it possible that there was something in the display area that was even *more* valuable than the ring, the belly-button jewel, and the missing third piece? Or could it be that the attempted theft was just some enterprising burglar trying to take advantage of Willis's permanent absence from the property? It left me with more questions than I'd had when I'd gone to sleep, so I hoped that Jake's presence would shed some light on just another odd occurrence over the last day.

To my surprise, I was just starting the cake donuts when Emma came in.

"You're early," I said as I glanced at the clock.

"I wanted to bring you up to speed on what happened after I left you yesterday," she said. "It might be easier to tell you before I clock in."

"I've got to admit that I've been curious," I told her as I worked. "I would have called, but I didn't want to be too nosy."

She shook her head. "I don't think you're nosy at all."

"Really? Not at all?" I asked lightly, trying to ease her clearly somber mood.

"Okay, maybe a little, but in a good way, you know?"

"I'll take it," I told her. "So, what happened?"

"I left you and found Mom. I laid everything out on the table, and I didn't hold anything back. She agreed with me one hundred percent, across the board. We decided that I didn't want him as a fiancé anymore, so we went to the restaurant to break up with him."

"Both of you? Together?" I asked her, glancing up from the old-fashioned donuts simmering away in the hot oil.

"I wanted to break up with him, but Mom also wanted to chew him out for the way he's been treating me lately. She figured as a co-owner, she'd kept quiet about it all too long."

"What happened? How did Barton take it?" I asked, pulling the donuts out at the perfect time, at least as far as I was concerned.

"I swear I don't think he cared, at least about me," Emma admitted a little sadly. "That was a little hard to take, but the next part was even worse."

"Worse than having your rejection rejected?" I asked as I dropped the next rounds of batter.

"I don't know; it was all pretty bad," she admitted. "He said that he'd outgrown us both anyway, as partners and me as a fiancé, and then he told us that he wanted to buy us out so he wouldn't have to see either one of us again."

"He doesn't have anywhere near that kind of money," I said, shocked that the man had let his ego flare up so wildly that he would turn his back on Emma and Sharon's generosity, not to mention my assistant's love she'd offered him so unwaveringly.

"He doesn't, but evidently, he knows someone who does," Emma said as she picked up one of the old-fashioned donuts I'd just glazed and started eating it. I didn't blame her. If I'd been in her shoes, I'd be stress eating, too. "We demanded to know who it was, but he wouldn't answer us right away, not until we gave him a number that we'd settle for."

"How could you possibly know how much you've put into the place so far?" I asked. Recordkeeping was not my strong suit, and I knew Emma had some issues with it as well.

"Momma knew to the penny how much we'd invested, both from our inheritance and from her retirement account."

"But surely all of the hours you both worked was a factor, too," I said.

"I wanted to forget that part, but Mom gave him a figure that added twenty thousand dollars over and above the amount we'd invested. She told me later that if we got it, we'd split it right down the middle."

"I still think he's getting off cheap," I said, but I was still happy that Sharon had added a financial assessment against Barton as a jerk tax. "What did he say?"

"He made a call, and then he told us that we'd have the check by nine a.m. this morning," she said.

"I can't believe how quickly it all came apart," I told her. "I'm so sorry."

"Do you want to know something? I'm not. He's changed so much I barely recognize him these days. If that's what having a restaurant does to him, I'm out."

"So, who is this mysterious backer?" I asked. Okay, my curiosity got the better of me, and I couldn't wait any longer to hear who it was.

"Do you remember he told me about a visitor he'd had earlier yesterday? It was his new angel, Helena Westinghaven."

"Helena?" I asked, shocked. "*She's* backing Barton?"

"Evidently," Emma said with a shrug.

"Well, she certainly has the money, but I had no idea she was interested in the restaurant business," I answered as I pulled another round of donuts out. "I thought she was into real estate."

"Well, she's interested in Barton, I think. The restaurant investment is just the way she's going to get him. I don't even mind the fact that she's thirty years older than he is or that she was a trophy wife who inherited her late husband's fortune. What I do mind is that I think he's been doing more than flirting with her for some time."

"Wow. I mean, wow. I don't know what else to say," I told her.

"I do," Emma said, biting her lower lip for a second.

"What's that?"

"Good riddance," she replied. "I've cried quite a few tears, and I'm sure I'll cry more, but this is the right thing for me, and it's the right thing for Mom, too."

"Hey, at least you're getting paid for *some* of the hours you've put in, too," I told her, amazed by the strength my young friend was exhibiting.

"Mom's going to use hers for travel, and I'm putting mine toward college," she said. "Anyway, with that distraction gone, I'll have more time to study and to work here, too."

"You know you'll always have a place here with me," I told her as she clocked in and started washing dishes. "Still, if you'd like to take a few personal days, I can handle things here at the donut shop."

"Actually, I think working is the best thing I can do right now," she answered. "Oh, I forgot to ask. Is it okay if I leave for an hour at nine and meet Mom and Barton at the bank?"

"Of course it is," I told her. "Is *she* going to be there?"

"Honestly, I couldn't care less," Emma said. After a moment, she added, "Okay, maybe I care a little. Since she's paying for everything, I suppose she'd have to be, wouldn't she? I should probably leave all of my sharp objects here with you before I go."

"And your Mace, too," I told her. "Don't forget that."

"Come on, can't a girl have *any* fun?" she asked me with a wry grin.

"Yes, but not *that* kind," I answered.

We took our break a little later, during which Emma most assuredly did not want to discuss her former fiancé, her former restaurant, and basically her former life. I was fine with that. I was there for her, but if she wanted to bottle it up or even bury it for the moment, that was good, too. We got back to making donuts soon enough, but Jake still hadn't called.

I was about to phone him ten minutes before we were set to open when my cell phone rang.

It was Jake, finally!

"Hey. Sorry it took me so long to get back to you, but after we looked around Willis's place, we decided to stake the place out just in case they came back."

"Did he? Or she, I guess?" I asked.

"Nope, but I think they did what they wanted to do and took off. Anyway, we grabbed an early breakfast before everyone else had to get to work, so I just got back home."

"How did they break in?" I asked.

"They busted out a window in the back of the house," Jake said as he stifled a yawn. The poor thing wasn't used to the hours I lived on a nearly daily basis, but then again, he'd gotten to bed after me and had been up two hours before.

"While you were there, did you happen to spot anything *else* that might be valuable?" I asked him. "Was there a reason the killer returned to Willis's house?"

"How could you possibly know what I was about to tell you next?" he asked me. "I was saving the best part for last."

"You found something else?" I asked, suddenly getting very excited.

"Not else. Something—actually three somethings—that were returned, not taken," he said.

"Okay, I'm not following you," I told him.

"Whoever broke in didn't *take* anything. They brought back the missing ring, the orange sculpture that we couldn't figure out was even missing, and the gem out of the dancer's belly button."

"The killer came back to *return* the things he took? Why kill Mitchell Willis in the first place, then?" I asked, trying to wrap my head around what had happened.

"That's what we're all trying to figure out," Jake admitted.

"So, that throws robbery out of the motive mix," I replied.

"Not necessarily," Jake answered. "They may have killed him for the valuables but then got overwhelmed with remorse over what they'd done and put them back."

"That wouldn't bring Willis back," I pointed out.

"Who knows what they were thinking. Anyway, I wanted you to know. Oh, by the way, Chief Holmes knew that you hadn't been in Willis's house before she let you and Grace go in with them."

That caught me off guard. "How could she possibly have known that?"

"She said it was clear the moment she asked you about it."

"Then why did she let us tag along?" I asked. Evidently I wasn't quite as good at lying as I'd thought I was.

"Partly to irritate Smiley," Jake replied. "But I also think she wanted to see if you two might spot something that everyone else missed. I know you don't have a very high opinion of Chief Holmes, but she has one of you and Grace. She knows exactly how good you two are at investigating. That request for information she gave you wasn't an indication of guilt. It was a sign of her respect. I think you're barking up the wrong tree there."

"So do I," I admitted.

"I'm sorry, what was that?" he asked.

"I've been thinking about it, and it just doesn't make any sense that Chief Holmes would do all of the things it would take to hide the murder, let alone show us into Willis's house. It just doesn't add up," I said.

"When did you come to that conclusion?" he asked me.

"When I was finishing up the cake donuts a little bit ago," I admitted.

"That's good. Then I don't have to tell you about her alibi, do I?" Jake asked, and I could hear the grin in his voice.

"She has an alibi?" I asked him.

"There was a wreck in town, and she was trying to sort out who was lying and who was telling the truth about what happened for over two hours, the hours in question, as a matter of fact," Jake said.

"Why didn't you lead with that information?" I asked him.

"I wanted to see if you'd had a chance to change your mind first."

"Well, I have, but I will admit that it's still good to get an alibi for her."

He chuckled a bit. "Belt and suspenders, right?"

"No way my pants are falling down if I can help it," I said with a smile of my own. Jake was about to say something when he yawned again. "You, sir, need to take a nap."

"I don't need one," he answered, yawning yet again. "Well, maybe a little one. Do you have a big day planned after you shut the donut shop down for the day?"

"Grace and I are going to keep digging," I admitted. "How about you?"

"I might find a way to make myself useful," Jake said.

"Then I'll touch base with you later," I told him as the clock hit 6 a.m., our opening time. "Time to sell the donuts."

"Talk to you later, Suzanne. Love you."

"Love you, too," I said, and then I opened the door to start a new day of donut peddling. I hadn't mentioned Emma's news to my husband for a couple of reasons. One, it wasn't mine to share with the world, and besides, Jake didn't need the distraction. He was protective of Emma, and I wouldn't have put it past him to go to Union Square and put a knot in Barton Gleason's tail if he knew the truth about what had happened.

The time for that had passed, anyway. Barton had clearly moved on, and Emma was doing her best to do the same.

Nobody needed my husband butting in.

Or me either, truth be told. Emma had handled things better than I would have if I'd been in her shoes, and I was proud of her.

If it had been me, I would have tried to get twenty thousand extra apiece just for the pain and suffering the unbearable chef had put everyone through lately.

Oddly enough, not many of my customers wanted to talk about the murder of the health inspector. Then again, I supposed it made sense. After all, he'd lived in Maple Hollow and had been murdered in Union Square, and though the three towns weren't all that far apart, most of the time, the folks of April Springs worried about things going on in *their* little town. Evidently, word hadn't gotten out yet about Emma and Barton, and I knew that as soon as it did, she'd be flooded with "sympathy" comments about the dead relationship, but it helped that Emma worked in back while I took care of our customers, so maybe it wouldn't be so bad.

At ten minutes before nine, Sharon came in, looking grim. I didn't have any customers at the moment, and Emma was still in the kitchen washing up.

"You can go on back," I told Sharon.

"Can you believe that loser?" she asked me, hesitating up front instead.

"Which part of it?" I asked.

"All of it," she replied.

"It honestly baffles me that *anyone* would be unkind to Emma for *any* reason," I told her honestly.

"I know, right? He's not the man I thought he was, that's for sure."

"Are you happy with the settlement you two are getting?" I asked her.

Sharon shrugged. "I wanted to ask for more for pain and suffering, but you know my daughter. She's got a good heart. Too good, some might say."

"I suppose if you're going to have a flaw, that's a pretty good one to have," I answered. "Want some coffee and a donut while Emma gets ready?"

"I don't think I could keep a thing down," she admitted. "Suzanne, is it wrong of me to be happy that this didn't work out? Not Emma and Barton, I mean the whole restaurant. I thought it was what I wanted, but I'm clearly not cut out for it."

"It's not for everyone," I admitted. "Still, you get to run Donut Hearts two days a week with your daughter, if you're still interested."

"I think it might be what saves her," Sharon said just as Emma came out.

"Saves who?"

"Me. You. All of us," Sharon said.

"Wow, that's a pretty big ask," she said with a shrug. "So, are you ready to get out of the restaurant business?"

"The question is, are you?" Sharon asked her.

"I won't be able to sign those papers fast enough to get him out of my life once and for all," Emma said firmly.

"After the money transfer is complete, though," Sharon said.

"Of course. Do you honestly think he'll try to cheat us?" Emma asked her mother.

"Absolutely. Don't you?"

"There's no doubt in my mind," Emma answered with a laugh. "That's why I'm so glad I've got you two in my corner."

"Hey, I didn't do anything," I told her. "This is all you."

"You've done more than you could ever know," Emma said, and then she gave me a brief but rather fierce hug. "Are you ready, Mom?" she asked after she broke free.

"More than I care to admit," Sharon answered.

"When we see you again in an hour, we'll be officially out of Twenty-First Southern," Emma said.

"We'll all have a donut and celebrate," I told her. "What about it, Sharon? Do you think you'll be able to eat then?"

She looked at the display case. "No, no donuts for me." I was about to protest when she added, "I would like seven bear claws and five apple fritters, though."

"Are you going to eat them here, or should I bag them up for you?" I asked her with a grin as I started collecting the requested treats.

"Let me start here, and we'll see how far I get," Sharon replied.

"That's my mom," Emma said, and then the two women took off for the bank to close out a part of their lives and, hopefully, open new ones.

Ten minutes after Emma and Sharon left, a nice looking young man in his early twenties with a backpack slung over one shoulder came into the shop.

"May I help you?" I asked him as he looked around.

"Yes, ma'am. I'd like a donut." He stared back toward the kitchen.

"Any kind in particular?"

"What? Oh, sure. Glazed would be good. Is there any chance Emma is here?"

"You just missed her," I told him.

"The story of my life," he said softly to himself. I wasn't supposed to hear it, but I did.

"How do you know Emma?" I asked as I put the donut on a small plate and then put it on a tray after taking his money.

"We have Econ 360 together," he said. As he took his change, he asked softly, "Is it true?"

"That my donuts are the best in North Carolina? I hate to brag, but I think they're special."

"I mean about Emma," he said, looking a bit embarrassed.

"I knew what you meant," I told him, giving him a gentle smile.

"Did she finally dump him? I've been wanting to ask her out from the moment I met her, but I took too long, and Barton swooped in. Am I really going to get a second chance with her?"

"That depends. Are you planning on breaking her heart, too?" I asked him.

"Me? No. No way. I think she's amazing! I would never hurt her."

I wasn't sure why, but I believed him. "I don't think you would. But you might want to give her some time to get over this before you ask her out."

"I appreciate the advice, but I already lost one chance with her because I waited too long. The second I see her, I'm asking her out."

"Good for you," I said as I grabbed another donut.

"I only wanted one," he said, looking a bit confused by my largesse.

"I know, but this one's on the house. Good luck."

"Thanks. So, when will she be back?"

I decided to give him one more piece of unsolicited advice. "She's not thinking straight right now. Barton burned her pretty badly. You should at least give her a month to come to terms with what happened."

He thought about it, and then he nodded. "I'm sorry. I truly am, but I can't do that. I can't wait a month, or even a week to ask her out. One day. But only one. She's too special a lady to stay free for very long. She can do whatever is best for her, but I need to tell her how I feel. I'm Jason, by the way, Jason Clover."

"I'm Suzanne Hart. It's nice to meet you, Jason."

He took a bite of donut, and then he grinned like a little boy. "Wow, you weren't kidding. This is amazing."

I knew there was a reason I liked him. "Thank you, Jason. Remember, one day."

"I'll see you tomorrow, Ms. Hart," he said with a grin. "You'll recognize me, because I'll be the one with flowers and candy. I know, it's kind of mushy and sentimental, but then again, I'm a mushy and sentimental kind of guy."

"There's nothing wrong with that," I said with a grin. "The world needs more mushy and sentimental right now."

"I couldn't agree with you more. I'll see you tomorrow," he said with a grin as he left, but not without grabbing his donuts first.

I had a hunch that I would, too.

I decided not to tell Emma about her visitor when she got back. She deserved a nice surprise, and even if she didn't end up going out with Jason, it was nice to be asked.

Emma and Sharon came back an hour later, almost to the minute. They'd both clearly shed some tears, but they also looked relieved by finishing with Barton Gleason once and for all. Sharon managed to put away two bear claws and a fritter while she was there, which was impressive enough, but she also asked for the remaining treats I'd set aside for her to be bagged so she could take them home with her. Emma laughed, said good-bye to her mom, and then she headed back to the kitchen to sink her arms into warm, soapy water and try to put what had happened behind her.

I had a hunch she was going to be just fine.

Chapter 17

"HEY, SUZANNE," JAKE said as he walked into the donut shop a little after ten.

"Hey yourself. I thought you were going to take a nap," I scolded him.

"I did. Two hours on the couch, and I'm a new man."

"I hope not. I'm kind of attached to the old one," I told him. "Would you like anything to nibble on?"

"I might take a few donut holes," he said.

"That's it?"

"Between your desserts, your mother's surprise treats, and now Phillip's peanut brittle, I'm putting on a few pounds I don't want."

"You look good to me," I said as I complied with his request. Well, almost. I put four donut holes in a bag, but four is a few, right?

"That's just one of the reasons I love you," he said as he peeked into the bag. I saw him count them, but if he minded the heavy hand, he didn't comment. "That's not the only reason I came by, though." He looked around and saw that the few customers I had were deep into their own conversations. There were times when I felt as though all of April Springs was hanging on my every word, but mostly, it was like this morning. I was the donut and coffee purveyor, and that was about it. "Can we talk?"

"I doubt you could get their attention with anything short of shooting off your gun," I told him. "But don't. I can't handle fleeing panic."

"You're safe with me, and you know it. It's about two of our suspects."

I loved how he said "our." "Which ones?"

"Willis's two supervisors, the ones with the newborn. They both have rock-solid alibis for the time of the murder," Jake replied.

"If you're satisfied, then I am," I said.

"Aren't you even curious?" he asked me.

"Of course I am, but I didn't want to push you on it," I replied with a grin.

"Since when?" he asked me, matching my smile with one of his own. "It turns out they were in the hospital with their newborn."

"Oh, no. Was it serious?"

"It was just a plain old rash, but they wouldn't budge until their pediatrician saw them, and he happened to be at the hospital at the time. Every nurse at the pediatric nursing station was willing to vouch for the fact that neither one of them left the waiting room, let alone the building, for the time in question."

"Hey, that's good news though, right?" I asked him as I refilled a cup of coffee for an older fellow new to town. He'd bought five donuts and some coffee after introducing himself, and I glanced over at him from time to time, watching him enjoy each and every bite of them, one at a time. He was definitely my kind of guy.

"It's very good news," Jake said, "though I'm still not at all sure Willis wasn't blackmailing them about something."

"What makes you say that?"

"How else could he act with such impunity if he didn't have an ace in the hole?" Jake asked. "Let's face it, getting fired from a government job isn't all that easy, but I have a feeling that doing what he was attempting to do would be enough."

"Are you going to look into it?" I asked him.

"It's not my problem," Jake said with a shrug, but I could tell from his expression that he was holding back on me.

"You've already spoken to someone, haven't you?"

"I happen to know a deputy sheriff, and I might have mentioned that something might be going on there, but that's all I can say," Jake admitted as he popped one of the donut holes into his mouth.

"You're just trying to hide your smile, aren't you?" I asked him playfully.

"No, these donuts are just that good," Jake answered, and I could see the hint of a grin forming before he squelched it. "Where does that leave you and Grace?"

"The same place you are," I answered. "We're still looking at Fred Ballantine, Smiley the pawnbroker, Gert Leister, Barton, and ...that's it."

"Go on, you can say her name," Jake said softly. "Sophia DeAngelis."

"I didn't say it. I'm not even going to think it," I told him.

"She *has* to be on your list of suspects, Suzanne, no matter how you feel about her and her family."

"That's where you're wrong, sir," I told him. "She can be on *your* list if you care to put her there, but I refuse to believe that Sophia did anything more than give the health inspector a gentle push."

"What if she killed him, though?" Jake asked again, much softer this time.

"Then it's going to be up to someone else to prove it," I told him flatly. "Because I'm certainly not going to."

Jake nodded. "Yeah, I thought you might feel that way, but unfortunately, the police don't have that luxury."

"But you're retired, remember?" I asked.

"I'm an unpaid resource in the investigation," Jake answered.

"Then that's on you, but you know where I stand."

"I do, now and forever," he said. "Hey, what's going on with Emma?"

I knew that gossip in April Springs traveled fast, but Jake had been asleep for most of the early-morning hours. "How did you find out what happened so quickly?"

"Find what out? I've just seen her peeking her head out of the kitchen three times since I got here. She's clearly waiting for someone to show up."

"Or trying to avoid them if they do," I countered.

"Okay, now I'm really intrigued."

I decided it would make my life too difficult to keep it from Jake any longer. Besides, I knew that he'd keep it to himself if I asked him to. "This is just between us, but she dumped Barton last night." I took a minute to catch him up on all of the details, including the sale of the property that had occurred less than an hour earlier.

"Good for her," Jake said when I finished, nodding his approval. "I always thought Emma was too good for him. But I didn't think Barton had two nickels to rub together. How did he manage to come up with enough cash to buy them out?"

"It wasn't Barton's money; it came from his backer, Helena Westinghaven," I told him. "Do you know her?"

"Just what I've heard around Union Square," he acknowledged.

"Can you believe she's spending that much money just to get to Barton?" I asked.

"I'm not one hundred percent sure that's what she did," Jake said after a moment.

"What do you mean?"

Jake bit his lower lip, and finally he said, "This is just between the two of us. You can't whisper a word to Emma or Sharon or anyone else. I came into some information quite by accident, and it could hurt the person who told me if word got out that I said anything."

I could see from Jake's expression that he was dead serious. "Now I'm the one who is intrigued. I won't breathe a word."

"It seems Helena is buying up some key Union Square real estate," Jake said. "She's been quietly acquiring properties around the restaurant, for what purpose I don't know. I have to wonder if *that's* why she's backing Barton, so she can shut him down and steal the spot out from under him."

"If that's what she's doing, it would serve him just right," I said. "Still, I hate to think that Emma and Sharon are missing out on an opportunity to make more money."

"I wouldn't let that worry me if I were you," Jake replied. "They're away from Barton, and they got their investment back plus something extra. In my book, they did just fine."

"I suppose that's true enough," I told him. "It would be poetic justice if Barton tried to squeeze Emma and Sharon out and ended up getting squeezed out himself."

"If there's any justice in the world, it would," Jake replied just as his cell phone rang. He glanced at the caller ID and said, "I've got to take this."

"See you later," I told him.

"Looking forward to it," Jake replied.

After he was gone, I thought about what he'd just told me. If it were true, and Helena had just strung Barton along in order to get the property where the restaurant was located, I'd try to act surprised when I found out.

We were half an hour from closing the shop for the day when a surprise visitor showed up at Donut Hearts.

"Fred Ballantine. What are you doing here?" I asked him with a smile.

"Since we met yesterday, I've been asking around. It seems as though everybody loves your donuts, so I wanted to see what I was missing."

"I'm sorry to say that none of them have any alcohol in them, so you might be disappointed," I told him with a smile.

"Yeah, about that. I want to apologize for the way I acted yesterday. Most days, I can handle my liquor just fine, but yesterday was not one of them."

"You had an excuse. You'd just lost a friend of yours."

He shook his head. "My *best* friend. Anyway, I lost my head, and I'm sorry you had to see it."

"Apology accepted," I said.

"Like I said, that wasn't me." After a moment, he looked at me directly and asked, "Have you had any luck finding out who killed him?"

"I understand the police are following lots of leads," I said neutrally.

"Yeah, well, the police can go climb a tree for all I care. I'm talking about you and your friend, Grace."

"It seems you've been asking around about more than my donuts," I told him, keeping my voice calm and level as I spoke.

"What can I say? I'm a talker, but I listen, too," he said. "Well? Have you?"

"We're making some progress," I admitted, though I wasn't entirely sure that was even true at this point. We were at the juncture where it felt as though all we did was spin our wheels, looking for some angle to wedge our way into the case. It happened that way more often than not, where one single clue opened the floodgates for everything we'd learned up to that point.

"Okay then," he said, and then he started to turn away.

"Fred, aren't you forgetting something?" I asked him.

"What's that?"

"Surely you didn't drive all the way to April Springs just to chat with me," I told him, though I suspected that was exactly why he'd come. "You came for some donuts, remember?"

"Oh, yeah. Give me a dozen," he said, clearly distracted by my direct approach.

"Is there anything you like in particular?"

"I trust you. Surprise me," he said as he reached for his wallet and tried to pull out a twenty. I say tried, because there was a homemade bandage wrapped around the knuckles of his right hand, and it was clearly sore as he wrestled with his wallet to extract a bill.

"What happened? Did you cut yourself?" I asked him, pushing the point home.

"No, I wasn't paying attention, and I slammed the car door on my hand," he said sheepishly.

I handed him the donuts and then tried to give him his change, but he just shook his head. "Put it on my tab."

"We don't run tabs," I told him pleasantly.

"Then stuff it in the tip jar," he said, grabbing his donuts and leaving. It seemed as though it was all he could do not to run out of the store once he had what he wanted from me, and I didn't mean the donuts.

"Jake, there's something you need to know," I said as I called my husband the moment Fred hurried out the door.

"What's up?"

"Fred Ballantine just left here. He came by the donut shop and tried to pump me for information," I told him.

"That doesn't mean he's guilty of anything more than being a gossip," Jake told me.

"Maybe not, but when he pulled his wallet out, I saw that he'd busted up his hand, and recently too. It was almost as though he broke a window last night, trying to get into someplace he shouldn't have been, you know?"

Jake laughed. "That I can use. Thanks for the tip."

"You are very welcome," I said. "Do you have anything for me?"

"Not yet, but I'll let you know," he answered, and then he hung up.

I didn't regret giving my husband the information. He and his police chief pals could apply pressure and get the real story out of Fred, while I had to depend on his cooperation. There were things that Grace and I did well and things the police were better equipped to handle. We wouldn't know the first thing about fingerprints or really anything forensic at all, but we were experts at getting people to say things they didn't mean to tell anyone else. Working together, it was amazing how anyone got away with murder in our little towns, though I was sure that it still happened.

I'd been planning on interviewing Fred before he'd waltzed into the shop, but I could take his name off our list, at least for now. That still left us with Smiley, Gert, and Barton. I wasn't in any mood to talk to the chef, so until we had something a little more concrete than what we had, I'd tell Grace that we needed to focus on Smiley and Gert. It wasn't that I didn't want to see Barton fry for the murder; it was mostly that I couldn't trust myself to be in his presence and not take a swing at him. He'd thrown away one of the best women I'd ever known, along with her mother and the chance of a lifetime to make a success with them, and I wasn't at all sure how I'd handle it the next time I saw him face to face.

Better to wait on that and go after the two suspects left that I wasn't tempted to run over with my Jeep.

Chapter 18

"HEY, SUZANNE. ARE you ready to roll?" Grace asked as she walked into Donut Hearts ten minutes before we were set to close for the day.

"You're early," I told her as I pointed to the clock on the wall.

"Emma can close up," she suggested. "I'm ready to get started."

"Not today she can't," I said softly.

"Why? What's up?"

"I take it you haven't heard the news," I told her in a near whisper.

"Not yet, but if I'm not about to, you and I are going to have a real problem."

"Emma broke up with Barton yesterday, and she and Sharon sold the restaurant to someone who's backing him instead," I told her quickly. The last thing I wanted was for Grace to say something inadvertently to Emma.

"Wow. A lot's been happening in the past twenty-four hours."

"Including a murder," I told her. "I'm guessing Stephen told you everything Jake told me, or am I wrong?"

"I can only assume what Jake told you, but yeah, I have a feeling we're on the same page. Who do we have left on our list that we can talk to today?"

"Smiley, Gert, and Barton," I said just as Emma walked up front.

"I think Barton did it," Emma said as she collected the rest of the dirty dishes and trays from up front.

"Do you honestly think he could have killed Mitchell Willis?" I asked her.

"A few months ago, I wouldn't have believed it was possible, but he's been acting so strange lately that I can't say one way or the other. Even if he hadn't been such a jerk to me lately, that's reason enough to break up with him, isn't it?"

"Considering him a murder suspect would certainly cause me to have some doubts," Grace said levelly.

"Grace," I chided her lightly.

"She's not wrong, Suzanne," Emma said with a shrug. "Be careful around him. I used to think I knew how he'd handle anything, but lately, I'm not so sure. If you back him into a corner, don't let him near any sharp knives, especially that butcher knife of his."

"Or frying pans," Grace said. "I want to talk to you about that, Suzanne."

"Don't mind me," Emma said as she took the bins in back. As the kitchen door closed, she added, "I'll be rocking my tunes, so feel free to speak freely."

"Wow, isn't she even grieving?" Grace asked a moment later.

"In her own way," I said, defending my young friend. "She's still processing it all, and I have a hunch she's just getting started on recovering from the blow of losing so much."

"Well, remind her that I'm here for her if she needs me," Grace answered. "I know you're one of her best friends, but we've all been burned by bad men in our lives before, and if I can help, I want to be there for her."

"That's sweet of you, but we've also had some pretty good experiences with them, too," I reminded her.

"I'm not about to argue that point," Grace said with a grin.

"You were talking about the frying pan before," I nudged her.

"Everybody is just assuming it was a frying pan, but could it have been something else?" she asked me.

"I suppose so, but since Mitchell Willis dealt with people in the food-service industry, it just makes sense that it's something like that. I suppose it could be a bacon press or even a doorstop when it comes down to it."

"How about the flat part of a butcher's knife?" she asked me with one arched eyebrow.

"I suppose it's possible," I said, remembering how the chef had threatened us with the very same instrument the day before.

"Yeah, but it's probably a frying pan," Grace admitted. "I just hate when everybody assumes one thing and it turns out to be something else. This way, if we find a different murder weapon, I come out of it looking like some kind of genius."

"You look like one to me, anyway," I told her.

"Because of the people I hang around with?" Grace asked me with a grin.

"That could certainly be one reason," I told her. "I'm going to need around twenty minutes until I'll be ready to go sleuthing. Is there something else you can do in the meantime?"

She looked at the donuts still on the display racks. "I might be able to find a way to keep myself occupied." After a minute, she asked, "What, no crullers or bear claws left?"

"I had a good supply of both earlier, but Sharon pretty much wiped me out," I told her.

"Sharon? As in Emma's mom, Sharon?" Grace asked me.

"The very same. Why?"

"It just seems to me that if she had a craving for those treats, she could wait until she and Emma were running the joint and make all she wanted," Grace answered.

"True, but a craving is pretty hard to predict. Is there anything else that might do instead?"

Grace shrugged. "Maybe I can make up for quality by opting for quantity. Bring me three of your favorite donuts."

"Get them yourself," I told her with a smile as I handed her a nitrile glove.

"Hey, is that any way to treat a paying customer?"

"I'm sorry, I misunderstood you. Does that mean that you're actually paying?" I asked her with a smile.

She laughed. "Touché. Give me the glove."

"With pleasure," I told her as we both started laughing.

Precisely at eleven, Emma came out of the kitchen. "Are you finished with that plate, Grace?"

There were still pieces of two donuts on it.

"What do you think?" she asked with a sickly smile.

"I think that plate can wait until tomorrow to wash," she answered in kind. "Suzanne, Mom wants me to go over some paperwork we need to shred about the restaurant. Do you mind if I skip out now?"

"Skip away," I told her. Changing my tone of voice, I added, "If you need me, call me. If it's late, call me. If it's early, call me. If it's somewhere in between..."

"I know. Call you," Emma said with a nod. "Got it."

"The same goes for me," Grace said.

"Thanks, ladies. I appreciate that."

After she left, I locked the doors behind her and got to work. "Feel free to grab a broom," I told Grace. "It will get us out of here faster."

"I'm not in that big a hurry," she said as she took another bite. "What are you going to do with the three dozen donuts you have left?"

"I don't have any plans for them. Why, do you want them?"

"I thought we might use them on Gert and Smiley like the old days when we bribed suspects to talk to us for donuts."

"That sounds like a good plan, but why not Barton, too? After all, we have three dozen."

"He doesn't deserve your donuts," she said firmly.

"I agree. I just wanted to see what *you'd* say," I told her as I boxed them up. "I'm sure we'll find *some* use for them."

"I'm sure we will," Grace said as she grabbed one of the boxes and started rooting around in it.

"Hey, I thought those were for our investigation," I reminded her.

"Two of them are. I was led to believe that the third one was up for grabs."

"Grab away," I said as I started running the cash register report. Thankfully, the till balanced out, so we were out of the shop three minutes earlier than I'd first predicted.

"*Now* can we start grilling people?" Grace asked.

I held up the bank deposit bag. "As soon as we drop this off, we'll be ready," I said.

Once we were on the road to Maple Hollow, Grace asked, "Who is first on our list?"

"Since the county government offices are between April Springs and Maple Hollow, I figured we'd stop and talk to Gert Leister first."

"Do you have any ideas about what we should talk to her *about*? I mean besides asking her if she has an alibi for the time of the murder."

"I thought we'd dig a little deeper into her relationship with Mitchell Willis," I answered.

"She had a *relationship* with him?" Grace asked me, clearly incredulous about the thought.

"She told me he had a crush on her at one point, but I didn't say it was a romantic relationship," I told her. "After all, everyone who knows each other has *some* kind of relationship."

"They were coworkers," Grace said. "We know that much."

"That's why we're digging though, isn't it? To find out if she really had more than that with him. He didn't just give her that jewelry because they were buddies."

There was a young man at Gert's desk when we walked into the reception area, and he looked lost as he tried to juggle the phones and speak to us at the same time.

"Where's Gert?" I asked him as he took a breath before answering another call.

"The redhead? She called out sick today, and they stuck me here."

"She's not a redhead. She has jet-black hair," I told him. The guy was clearly frazzled.

"Whatever. All I know is that she left me holding the bag, and I don't have a clue what I'm doing. Man, my uncle is going to kill me."

"Who is your uncle?" Grace asked him, no doubt out of curiosity more than anything else.

"Storm Butcher," he said.

"Storm Butcher, the head of the county board of governors?" I asked.

"Yeah, that's him," he admitted.

"I think you'll be okay," I told him.

"Yeah, Uncle Storm did tell me I'd have to pretty much set the place on fire to get fired. Ha. I didn't mean the wordplay, but that's kind of funny."

Maybe so, but it wasn't my kind of funny. "Do you have any idea where Gert might be?"

"Home? The doctor? The lake? How could I possibly know?" he asked, and then he picked up another line and spoke. "Hold on one second, I'll put you through," he said as he pushed a button on his phone. "Man, I hung up on another one," he said with a shrug.

"We'll let you get back to it. Tell your uncle we said hello," Grace said.

"And you are?"

"I'm Breezy, and she's Sunshine," Grace answered with a straight face.

He diligently wrote our pseudonyms down. "I'll let him know."

"Good man," Grace said, and it was all we could do not to start laughing until we were safely out of the building.

"So, do you think Gert is really sick?" Grace asked me once we were outside.

"I kind of doubt it unless something came over her all of a sudden. She seemed perfectly fine yesterday."

"Then let's track her down at her place and see what she's really up to," Grace said.

"Let's make that our Plan B," I told her. "I'd like to talk to Smiley first, and then we'll see if we can find out where Gert lives."

"Oh, we'll find out all right," Grace said.

"You sound pretty confident about that," I told her as I started driving the rest of the way to Maple Hollow.

"That's because I'm going to ask my little friend," she said as she waved her phone in the air. "She knows everything."

"I didn't realize your phone was female," I told her.

"Doesn't it stand to reason she would be? After all, she's smart, dependable, and always there when you need her. That sounds like a woman to me."

"And, to be fair, some men," I told her.

"Yeah, but what fun would it be to call her a he?" Grace asked.

"Tell you what. While we're driving, go ahead and ask your girl where Gert lives, just in case."

"I can do that," Grace said, and sure enough, within five minutes, she had an address. "Are we going there first after all?"

"What part of Plan B do you not understand?" I asked her with a laugh.

"Hey, you've been known to change your mind, young lady."

"You don't have to remind me, but I still want to tackle Smiley first."

"I wouldn't mind tackling him myself, with a wrench or a pipe or maybe even a frying pan. That man gets on my nerves."

"Mine too, but maybe today, we can return the favor. Let's see how hard we can push him about his real relationship with Mitchell Willis. I still don't believe he just loaned him a fifty-thousand-dollar ring without paperwork or collateral or anything."

"Oh, goody, we can play bad cop, bad cop," Grace said, rubbing her hands together.

"I thought it was supposed to be good cop, bad cop."

"Fine, but you have to be the good cop," she told me firmly.

"Bad cop, bad cop it is," I replied.

When we walked into Smiley's pawnshop, we realized that we weren't going to get the chance to grill the broker after all, at least not until we could find him.

"We need to talk to Smiley," I told the man behind the counter.

"Yeah, and I need a million dollars. I'm afraid we're both in for disappointment today," the man said in a surly manner.

"What are you, his nephew?" I asked, based more on his disposition than his appearance.

"Yeah. What's it to you?"

"It's not," Grace said. "Come on, Suzanne. Let's go. See you later, bucko," Grace told him.

"It's not Bucko, the name's Hap, short for Happy," he corrected me.

"You could have fooled us," I replied.

"Is every one of our suspects ducking us today?" Grace asked me as we got back into the Jeep.

"Stephen told you that Fred came by the donut shop, right?" I asked.

"I'm talking about the two of us," she said. "Suzanne, are we just spinning our wheels? Stephen seemed to think Fred's busted hand was all he needed to arrest him."

"We both know better than that," I told her. "Sure, it doesn't look good for him, but we have other viable suspects, and until I hear they've got a confession, I vote we keep digging."

"I'm good with that," Grace said. "It does seem odd that he brought stuff back to the victim's house instead of taking more things."

"Maybe he has a guilty conscience."

"Maybe," Grace answered.

"But you don't think so, do you?"

"I don't know what to think at this point," Grace replied. "Here it is, just ahead. That's where Gert Leister lives."

"Hey, isn't that Smiley's truck parked in front?" I asked as I drove past the address Grace had given me earlier. "What's up with that?"

Grace looked back over her shoulder at the receding house. "I don't suppose we'll find out unless we actually go there and confront them."

"I wanted to sneak up on them," I admitted as I pulled the Jeep into an empty spot in a nearby parking lot. "Feel like walking back a hundred yards?"

"If I have to," Grace said with a feigned grimace.

"Think of it as walking off a bite of the donuts you had earlier," I told her.

"You think of it. Exercise just makes me want to eat. It's a vicious cycle these days."

When we got to Gert's front door, Grace leaned forward to ring the bell, but I grabbed her arm before she could.

"Listen. Did you hear that?" I asked her.

"No, I sure didn't," she admitted. "What did you hear?"

"It sounded as though two people were arguing," I told her.

"Then maybe we should listen some more and see what we can find out," Grace said.

"I couldn't have come up with a better plan myself," I told her with a wink.

"Hey, I never said it wasn't your plan in the first place," Grace replied, and then we both heard something that got our attention instantly.

Chapter 19

"I'M NOT GOING TO LISTEN to any more of this nonsense," Smiley said fiercely. "You are way off base, Gert."

"Why did you have to kill him, Smiley? What did he ever do to you? I wasn't the man's biggest fan, but surely his stuff wasn't enough reason to kill him!"

"I'm telling you once and for all, I didn't do it," Smiley snapped. "It was crazy coming here. You said you had something valuable for me, but you lied."

"I had to get you here to get the truth out of you," Gert protested.

"You wouldn't know the truth if it came up and bit you on the hindquarters," Smiley said as he pulled the door open unexpectedly and caught us clearly eavesdropping on their conversation. "Has every woman in the world suddenly gone crazy, or is it just the three of you?" Smiley asked as he rushed past us. "Hap told me you were at my shop again, looking for me. I'm going to tell you what I just told Psycho in there. I didn't kill Mitchell Willis. I just want my stuff back, and I'll be happy never to see any of you again."

"Didn't you hear?" Grace asked him. From her wicked grin, I knew what she was going to say next, but I didn't even try to stop her. I wanted to see how Smiley would react to the news.

"Hear what?" Smiley snapped.

"The ring and the belly-button gem were both returned to Mitchell Willis's house last night, along with an orange sculpture that had to be the third missing piece."

"What? Who would do something so stupid? That stuff had to be worth over a hundred thousand dollars altogether!"

"Somebody with a guilty conscience, maybe?" I asked him.

"Well, you can be sure I didn't do it! If I'd had my ring back, I certainly wouldn't put it back where I couldn't get to it again."

"I'm surprised you aren't claiming the other two pieces belong to you, too," Grace said sharply.

"Hey, contrary to what you apparently think, I'm no thief. I just want what's mine."

"Where are you going? Back to the pawnshop?" Gert asked him from the porch where she'd joined us.

"I'm going to the cops to start the paperwork on getting my ring back," Smiley said. "Not that it's any of your business."

"Which one of us are you referring to?" I asked him sweetly.

"All three of you," Smiley said, and then he got into his truck and took off.

I was about to ask Gert for an alibi when she slammed her front door shut. She was carrying that monster of a purse with her, and she almost knocked me off the porch with the blasted thing.

"Where are you going?"

"I don't believe him," she said as she raced for her car. "He's up to something, and I mean to find out what it is."

Suddenly, Grace and I were all alone again. "Should we follow them?" Grace asked me.

I was about to answer when my cell phone rang.

"It's Barton," I told Grace. "What should I do?"

"See what the weasel wants," she suggested. "But Suzanne, don't lose your cool just yet. Let's give him enough rope and see if he hangs himself with it."

"Hey, Barton, I don't have a whole lot of time. What can I do for you?"

"It's what I can do for you," he said. "I know I'm not your favorite person in the world right now, but I've got something at the restaurant that's going to blow the case wide open."

"We're in Maple Hollow," I told him.

"I'll wait, but you need to hurry."

Before I could ask him what he had, he hung up on me.

I called him back, but it went straight to voicemail.

"What was that all about?" Grace asked me.

"He says he's got something for us," I told her. "I don't believe him, though."

"What do you think he's doing, luring us to Union Square to knock us off, too?" she asked sardonically.

"I don't know what he's up to," I said as I headed back down the street to where we'd parked my Jeep.

"But we're going anyway, right?" she asked me.

"Unless you've got a better idea," I told her. "We've already lost Smiley and Gert."

"Let's go see what the weasel wants, then."

"We're going to need to stop for gas first," I said once we were in the vehicle. "All this running around is keeping my tank thirsty for more."

"Tell you what. This tank is my treat," Grace said.

"You don't have to do that."

"I know I don't have to. I want to."

"Well, I'm not about to argue with you," I said.

Once we'd topped off my gas tank, we headed to Union Square yet again.

As we drove, Grace and I discussed Barton's questionable sanity in dumping Emma, the case we were working on, the state of our husbands' relationship with each other, and anything else we could think of to pass the time.

By the time we finally got to Union Square, I was just ready to go off on Barton, no matter what he had for us. Unless it was the murder weapon and a signed confession, I wasn't planning to take it easy on him, not after what he'd done to Emma and Sharon with the restaurant and Emma with her heart.

"What's so important that we had to drop everything and rush right over here?" I asked Barton as we walked into Twenty-First Southern. Then I looked around. There were boxes everywhere, and the tables and chairs were shoved to the side. "What's going on?"

"Helena double-crossed me," Barton said, clearly on the verge of tears. "She told me once she had the building in her name, she was finished with me."

"What's going to happen to your restaurant?" Grace asked him, not even trying to hide the satisfaction in her voice.

"It's over," he said. "Suzanne, you have to help me get Emma back. I made one mistake! Surely she can forgive me if you tell her to."

I looked at him incredulously before I trusted myself to speak. "*One* mistake? You're kidding, right? You've been a complete and total jerk to her for months! *One* mistake? Really?"

He looked surprised by my declaration. "I know I haven't been the most attentive fiancé lately, but surely, she can understand the pressure I was under to make a go of it."

"Do you honestly think that *you* were the only one under pressure?" I asked him, taking a step closer to him. "They put *everything* on the line to make your dream come true, and what thanks did they get? You betrayed them! Barton, you have a serious disconnect with reality if you believe you made only one mistake!" I turned to Grace. "Do you have anything to add?"

She just smiled and shook her head. "No, ma'am. You're doing great all on your own."

"So you aren't going to help me win her back?" he asked me petulantly.

"No, I'm not," I said. "So, where's this supposed evidence you've got for us?"

"I was just trying to get you here. It was the only way I could get you to come," he said, acting like a little boy flippantly trying to justify his atrocious behavior.

"We're done here," I said to Grace.

As we were leaving, Barton said, "Tell Emma I'm leaving the area. I've got a job offer in Chicago to run a first-class restaurant there, and I'm going to take it."

Grace turned back and shook her head. "She doesn't care."

"Suzanne?" he asked.

"Emma," I answered for her. "Just go. Enough with the dramatics."

He frowned as we walked out, probably expecting us to try to stop him. Fat chance of that ever happening. Barton had shown his true colors once he thought he was getting his own restaurant. Or maybe his ego had been growing all along, and he'd turned into this ugly excuse for a man. But no matter what the reason, he'd lost his last chance with Emma, so leaving was probably the best thing for everyone.

Once we were back in the Jeep, I told Grace, "I need a shower after that."

"I know exactly what you mean," she said. "Hey, we're awfully close to Napoli's. Don't you think they'd like an update on what's been going on?"

"You don't just happen to want to eat there too, do you?" I asked her with a slight smile.

"Two birds, one stone, you know? Why not?"

I thought about going back there again, about the pain I was beginning to associate with the place. In all honesty, I hadn't planned on going back until this entire mess was settled, but maybe being with Angelica and her daughters was exactly what I needed at the moment.

"Sure, why not?" I asked mildly as I headed over there.

"Wow, try to rein in your enthusiasm," Grace said.

"It's complicated," I told her.

"That's why you need to face it now, before things get so awkward that you can *never* go back," Grace answered wisely.

"You're not hungry at all, are you? This was your plan all along."

"You take that back," she said with mock severity. "I'm *very* hungry."

"But the rest of it is true too, isn't it?" I asked as I pulled into the parking lot.

"Maybe," she said.

"It's okay to admit it. You're right."

"I'm not even going to gloat that you just admitted that," Grace said with a hint of aloofness in her voice.

"Not even a little?" I asked her.

"Well, maybe a little," she said, and then we both started laughing. I'd done well choosing my best friend in life, an amazing feat given the fact that the choice had been made in early childhood. That's just the way things went sometimes, and I was the better person for it.

"Mom wants you in the kitchen," Antonia said the second we walked in the front door.

"How did she even know we were coming?" I asked. "We just decided to drop in thirty seconds ago ourselves."

"We all have standing orders. If and when you show up, you are to be taken directly to the kitchen, with no excuses accepted." Antonia paused, and then she added softly, "Don't worry. It's a good thing."

"That's excellent, because I could use something good about now," I told her.

We followed Antonia into the kitchen, and the second Angelica saw us, she gave the spoon in her hand to Sophia and rushed toward us. Before I could say a word, she hugged me fiercely, which, coming from her, was saying something. "Suzanne, you have to forgive me. You just have to."

"We already cleared that up, remember?" I asked as I tried unsuccessfully to pull away.

"I know we said we did, but I didn't feel it."

"Well, you're not going to feel much more of me than you are now," I said, struggling for breath.

"Mom, let her at least breathe," Sophia said with a giggle.

"I'm sorry. My emotions get the better of me sometimes. Please tell me that you two are hungry."

"Well, *I* could eat," Grace admitted.

Angelica looked at my friend and smiled. "Hello, Grace. Would you like a hug as well?"

"I'm good," she answered as she sniffed the air with great appreciation. "I wouldn't mind trying whatever that is that smells so amazing, though."

Angelica laughed. "Sophia, the taste testers have arrived."

"Are you going to experiment on us?" I asked as I was finally released from her embrace.

"Only in a good way," she said as Sophia set the chef's table in the kitchen, where we'd eaten a great many times before.

"What is this?" Grace asked as Angelica put two plates in front of us.

"Sophia and I have been working on a new dish. We don't even have a name for it yet."

Grace took a bite, frowned for a moment, and then she said with all seriousness, "I'd call it a taste of heaven if I were you."

I took a bite myself and nodded my agreement. "This is amazing!"

"I told you, Mom," Sophia said triumphantly. "It's perfect just the way it is."

"It's good, but we can make it better," Angelica said after a moment.

"If you make it any tastier than it is right now, I'm leaving Stephen and moving into that corner over there," Grace said as she pointed to one edge of the kitchen.

"Maybe it's good enough, then," Angelica said, and we all started smiling and laughing.

Grace had been right. I'd needed this more than I'd realized.

We were just finishing up when I got a call.

"It's Jake," I said as I stood. "Do you mind if I take this out back?"

"Please, feel free," Angelica said.

"I'll watch your plate while you're gone," Grace said as she reached for what little I hadn't eaten yet.

"Don't worry, there's more where that came from," Angelica said.

I was laughing as I picked up. "Hey, Jake. What's up?"

"Wow, you sound like you're having too much fun without me," he said with a hint of joy in his voice.

"Grace and I are at Napoli's. You've got to try the new dish Sophia and Angelica are working on. It will blow your socks off."

"I look forward to being sockless," he said. "I've got some news, but it has to be quick."

"What's going on?"

"Chief Holmes just arrested Fred for the murder of Mitchell Willis."

"What? Did he confess?" I asked.

"Not to the murder, but he finally admitted that he was the one who returned the valuables last night. That was a good catch on the bandage."

"But why would he admit to that and not killing Willis?" I asked.

"Sometimes suspects do that. Maybe he figured that by pleading to the lesser charge, he'd skate on the murder."

"But you don't think so," I told him.

"Honestly, I don't know," Jake said. "Chief Holmes has asked Chiefs Erskine and Grant to join her in the interrogation."

"But not you?" I asked.

"Me, too. That's why I'm calling. We'll all be out of touch for the next few hours, trying to sweat a confession out of Fred Ballantine." I was about to say something when someone called his name from afar. "I've got to go. Don't hold dinner for me, not that you'll have any room left after what you're eating now."

"What was that all about?" Grace asked the moment she saw my face.

"The Maple Hollow police just arrested Fred Ballantine for Mitchell Willis's murder," I told her.

"That sounds like *good* news to me. So why aren't you smiling?"

"I don't know. I just didn't have things figured out that way," I admitted.

"Hey, even the greats get it wrong sometimes. Stephen likes to say that batters that strike out two out of three times at the plate still make it into the hall of fame."

"I guess you're right," I said.

Angelica clapped her hands. "So, the cloud is not over my Sophia anymore?"

"It never was, in our minds," I told her.

"I knew that, Suzanne. You are a dear friend to me, a sister I never had," Angelica said. "I'm sorry if I don't tell you that enough."

"You show your love in other ways that count," I said with a grin.

"With food, you mean?" Sophia asked happily.

"With friendship," I corrected her.

"Friendship *and* food," Grace added. "We can't leave food out."

I laughed along with them. "Well, I hate to eat and run, but we need to get back to April Springs. Thanks for the delicious meal and the even better company."

"You are both always welcome here," Angelica said with a smile.

And I knew that this time, she meant it with all of her heart.

All was right with the world again, at least this corner of it, and for me, that was all that really counted. It didn't matter whether Grace and I found the killer or someone else did, as long as the culprit was caught and punished.

At least that's what I kept telling myself as I drove us back to April Springs.

Chapter 20

AS WE GOT TO THE JUNCTION of Springs Drive and Viewmont Avenue back in the heart of April Springs, a right would have taken us to our homes. It was clear that was what Grace was expecting me to do.

I even expected it myself until, at the last second, I took a left.

"Suzanne, is there something you're not telling me?" Grace asked curiously beside me.

"I want to go to Maple Hollow one more time," I said as I continued on.

"Funny, but I thought we both had enough of that town for a while, especially since they've caught Willis's killer."

"I'm not so sure they have, though," I told her.

"Do you think Smiley did it?"

"No, I'm thinking it was Gert Leister," I said.

"Gert? Really? She's been fourth out of five on my list. First there's Fred, then Smiley, then Barton, and then Gert."

"Sophia actually made your list?" I asked her.

"Hey, I don't like it any more than you do, but I figured we had to include her just to be fair. Gert, huh?"

"Remember what that substitute clerk called her?" I asked.

"He said she was the redhead," Grace allowed. "But the guy was clearly scatterbrained. She has jet-black hair, and we both know it."

"That's what her hair color is *now*," I said. "Who knows how long it's been that way, though."

"Do you honestly think she dyed it red just to get Mitchell Willis's attention?" Grace asked me. "Again, I have to wonder why. Mitchell Willis was not what you'd call an attractive man by anyone's definition."

"No, but he had some awfully valuable gems in his possession. What if Gert overheard him bragging to Fred at work about his collection? Everyone knew about Mitchell's obsession with all things orange, and some redheads actually have orange hair."

"I suppose," Grace allowed.

"Hey, she hocked a piece of jewelry to Smiley that she admitted came from Mitchell," I reminded her. "What if that was just the tip of the iceberg?"

"How about this? What if Mitchell never gave it to her in the first place," Grace said, getting into the spirit of the idea. "She could have gone to his place and stolen it earlier."

"If she did that though, why didn't she go for the grand prize, that orange gem ring?"

"She knew he'd notice that immediately," Grace said with more enthusiasm. "The gem she pawned could have been a test to see how much she could get away with."

"So, is that why she killed Mitchell? Supposedly killed him, I should say?" I added, though it was just the two of us guessing about possible killers and their motives.

"What if he caught her in the act?" Grace asked me. "He would be furious, and she could have hit him with a frying pan to shut him up from telling everyone what she'd done."

"Oh. My. Lands."

"What? What is it? Are you having a stroke?"

"We've been looking at this all wrong from the very beginning. All of us," I said as I started to drive a little faster.

"How do you mean? Are you saying now that Gert *didn't* kill Mitchell Willis?"

"I still think she did it, but she didn't use a frying pan. Mitchell's job as a health inspector threw everyone off. Naturally, a food-related item made sense, but think about it. We've seen something more than once in the past twenty-four hours that could present a blow in the same way a frying pan might."

I waited for her to get it, and sure enough, less than ten seconds later, Grace said, "She hit him with her purse."

"Exactly. That thing has two flat sides that are made of metal! If she swung that at Mitchell's head, it would surely be enough to kill him. Call Stephen."

Grace tried, but there was no answer. "He's with the other chiefs, grilling the wrong man."

"Try Jake, Chief Holmes, and Chief Erskine too," I suggested.

She started dialing, but she came up empty. "Jake didn't pick up, and neither did Chief Holmes. It didn't do us a whole lot of good when she gave us her personal cell phone number. I don't have Chief Erskine's number, but I've got a feeling his ringer is off, too. Should we call the Maple Hollow police department and get someone else to talk to Gert?"

"No, on the face of it, it sounds kind of crazy. Let's see if Gert cracks if we push her a little harder. Once we have more evidence, we can turn her over to the authorities."

As we neared her place, Grace asked, "You know we're doing something we swore we'd never do again, don't you?"

"What, confronting a killer without backup? You're mine, and I'm yours. That should count for something."

"I admire your faith in us, but I'm not sure I share it."

"Should we not do this?" I asked as a car sped past us going the opposite way. I hit the wheel hard and nearly rolled my Jeep over despite its ability to handle such maneuvers. "That was Gert Leister," I shouted.

"Don't let her get away, then," Grace encouraged me.

"I won't if I can help it," I said. I followed her car, matching her pace and wondering where all of the Maple Hollow patrol officers were. We were going a good twenty miles over the speed limit, and when Gert realized we were on her tail, she sped up even more. She kept glancing back at us in her rearview mirror, and that turned out to be her downfall.

She was watching us when she should have been watching the road ahead of her.

It took a sharp turn, but Gert did not.

Her car rammed into three trees before coming to a full stop, and it was all I could do not to follow suit.

I jumped out of the Jeep and raced toward the car as I told Grace, "Call 911!"

When I got there though, the driver's-side door was standing wide open, and I heard a revolver hammer click behind me. "You couldn't leave well enough alone, could you? You made me wreck my car!" Gert screamed at me as blood dripped down her face into one eye. "Why were you following me?"

"I couldn't let you escape," I told her, hoping that she didn't see Grace as she crept toward us following the tree line, hopefully out of sight.

"Escape what?" she asked. "I didn't do anything."

"Give it up, Red," I told her. "We know."

She shook her head. "My hair is clearly black."

"Today maybe, but how about yesterday morning? Do you honestly think it will be that difficult to find someone to verify that you changed your hair color *after* Mitchell Willis was murdered?"

She shrugged. "I got tired of it, so I made a change. It's not against the law."

"No, but murder is." I pointed to the purse draped over one of her free hands. "In fact, that's the murder weapon right there."

She shook her head. "You can't prove that."

"I don't have to. Do you honestly think you got every scrap of DNA off of it? I can't imagine you were good enough to beat modern forensics."

Gert Leister looked doubtful, and I wondered where Grace was. I wasn't sure how much longer I could stall the killer before she pulled that trigger.

"If they don't test it, they'll never know," she said with a smile that sent chills through me. "Sorry, Suzanne, but you're just collateral damage."

At that moment, Grace shrieked from behind Gert, but she was too far away. As the killer swung her weapon around to shoot my friend, I knew it was make-or-break time.

I had half a second to act, or Grace was going to be dead.

Chapter 21

I THREW MYSELF AT GERT, and she reacted just the way I'd hoped she would. Instead of following through and shooting Grace first, she turned the gun back toward me.

But she was too late.

I knocked her to the ground as the first and only shot went into a nearby tree, and Grace grabbed the gun as I pinned Gert Leister to the ground.

Chapter 22

"GET OFF ME!" SHE PROTESTED.

"Not on your life," I answered, driving her deeper into the dirt.

Just then, we heard a police siren in the background, and all of the fight went out of the killer.

"He rejected me. Me. I couldn't believe it," she said coldly.

"What happened? Did he catch you stealing from him?" I asked her.

"I told him I was just trying it on to cover for it, but he said I wasn't a true redhead and that I should go! He said he didn't want to have anything else to do with me ever again. He called me cheap! I'm a lot of things, but cheap isn't one of them."

"So you killed him for *that*?" I asked, incredulous despite what I'd seen in the past with other killers. Who knew why certain things set them off? I'd leave that to the clinical psychologists. As far as I was concerned, the woman was crazy, plain and simple.

"I mean, look at *me*, and look at *him*! There was no *way* I was going to let him dump me!"

"But you didn't care about him, anyway," Grace said from above her.

"No, but he didn't know that! I lost my cool, I admit it. I didn't even realize how hard I hit him until he fell over, dead!"

"So you dumped the body in Union Square? What sense did that make?"

"I met him there, you moron. I didn't dump him anywhere!"

Okay, so maybe I'd missed the mark on that one, but I'd caught the killer, and that was a big point in my favor. As the cop approached, I stood up while Grace handed him the gun.

"She killed Mitchell Willis," I told him.

He shook his head. "Haven't you heard? Fred Ballantine did it."

"That's what I kept trying to tell them, Officer," Gert said, laying it on so thick she needed a trowel. "They ran me off the road and then abducted me! Arrest them! They hurt me!"

Before he could buy into her act, I said, "Hold on there one second. I'm married to Jake Bishop, and she's married to Chief Stephen Grant. Maybe you'd better call them before you do anything that's going to end your career."

"They're lying," she said as she moved closer to the cop. He probably thought she was doing it for protection, but I had a feeling she wanted that gun back. After all, what are three more kills after the first one? "I'm feeling faint. Catch me."

"Don't let her get that gun!" I shouted as she lunged for it.

The police officer took a step back and shoved her to the ground as he finally pulled his own weapon. "Nobody move!"

The young cop tried to hold his gun on all three of us, but Grace and I weren't about to move.

Not to run away, at any rate.

All I did was put my tennis shoe in the middle of Gert's back again.

There was no way she was getting back up on my watch this time.

Chapter 23

"WILLIS'S DNA WAS ALL over that purse," Chief Holmes said a little later as Chief Grant and Jake stood a few steps behind her. "She's
confessed to killing him."

"Good," I said. "How about Fred? Is he going to jail, too?"

"We could press charges, but we're not going to," she said. "It turns
out he was telling the truth about Mitchell Willis. He really was his
best friend. The murder victim left everything to him, so legally, he was
stealing his own stuff and then putting it back."

"How did the belly dancer end up in Union Square, then?" I asked.

"He told us that he knew Smiley would recognize it," Jake explained, "so he couldn't pawn it in town, so he drove to a jewelry shop
in Union Square. When he got near the front door, he knew that he
couldn't go through with it, so he headed back to his car. He dropped
it getting in, though, and all he could retrieve was the gem before you
two spotted him."

"Fred was *there* when we were?" I asked.

"So he says, and it all makes sense. The whole collection is his anyway, so it doesn't matter that he broke the dancer in the end."

"Smiley claims otherwise, at least about that expensive ring," I reminded her.

"Let them sort it out in court, because I don't care. I've got your
statements, so you two can go." As we started to walk out, she added,
"Thanks for your help on this one."

"Anytime, Chief," I told her.

"Let's not make a habit of it if it's all the same to you," she answered
with a grin.

"Hey, I'm just a simple donutmaker," I told her.

"We all know better than that. You and Grace make quite the
team."

"We do our best," I said.

"Which is usually pretty darn good," Grace echoed.

"Hey, Suzanne, can I get a lift back to April Springs?" Jake asked me with a smile.

"You'll have to ask Grace," I told him, matching it with one of my own.

"I'm riding with the chief, so you can have my spot," Grace said. She stopped and hugged me first, though. "We did it again, partner."

"I couldn't have done it without you," I told her.

"Right back at you."

"I just have to get something from the car, and we can go," Jake said.

He got into the passenger seat of my Jeep and opened a Tupperware container.

"What's this? Did Phillip make more peanut brittle?" I asked as I took a bite. It was every bit as good as the last batch.

"No, this one is all mine," he said proudly.

As I drove us home, I said, "Good job, sir. You now have two jobs in the kitchen: chili and peanut brittle."

"I wonder how chili peanut brittle would be?" he asked aloud.

"You can have all you want, but I'm not touching it with a ten-foot pole," I told him.

"Coward," he said with a grin.

"About some things? You betcha," I told him.

"You're brave in every way that counts, though," Jake replied.

"Coming from you, that's high praise," I told him.

We made the rest of the drive chatting about the most inane things, but it felt as though I was truly home whenever I was with my second—and by far my best—husband. I was sorry that Emma had lost what she'd thought she'd had with Barton, but I had every confidence that someday, she'd find what she was looking for, too.

It didn't take a man to make me complete, but there were times when it surely was nice having him around.

RECIPES

Microwave Peanut Brittle Recipe

Yes, you really can make peanut brittle in a microwave oven! Not just any brittle either, but the best peanut brittle I've ever had in my life! I've found this recipe online on three or four different sites, and I adapted, developed, and combined them as my own, so it couldn't be simpler. Plus it's great fun to make.

I used to make stovetop brittle, but never again, not after finding this recipe! We like to store this in wide-mouth mason jars with plastic screw-top lids, one of our favorite ways to store any and just about all candy, both homemade and store bought.

Ingredients

½ cup light corn syrup

1 cup granulated white sugar

1 cup dry-roasted lightly salted peanuts

2 dashes of salt

½ cup unsalted butter, room temperature

1 ½ teaspoons vanilla extract

2 teaspoons baking soda (It's important that this is fresh, so open a new box if you need to. It's inexpensive, and you can use the old stuff on a plate in your fridge or freezer, or wash it down the drain with hot water to freshen your pipes.)

Directions

In a large 8-cup measuring cup or large glass bowl with tall sides, stir in the corn syrup, white sugar, peanuts, and salt until well mixed.

The narrower base and taller sides make the measuring cup ideal so the brittle doesn't burn.

Microwave for 4 minutes, then remove it and stir, being careful because the bowl is starting to really heat up.

Microwave this mix for another 4 minutes, and as you're waiting, clean your spatula and wait patiently.

After this session, remove the cup or bowl from the microwave carefully (it is HOT now) and stir in the butter and vanilla. The butter doesn't have to incorporate completely, but it should all be melted.

Microwave 2 more minutes.

While it's on the last step, take a large cookie sheet and spread enough butter on it to keep the brittle from sticking.

Take the bowl out carefully (it's still HOT) and stir in the baking soda, stirring it in thoroughly. Be careful, it will foam up some, so be ready! Once it's all incorporated and light and fluffy (you need to act quickly here), spread the mix onto the cookie sheet as thin as you can get it and as fast as you can do it. This all has to be done very quickly, but be careful, because, you guessed it, it's very HOT!

Let the brittle cool, and then break it up into whatever size pieces you prefer.

Store the brittle in jars with lids, and enjoy.

Makes three one-quart wide-mouth mason jars of brittle.

Wonderful Baked Chocolate Cake Donuts

I love chocolate donuts, and this is my favorite recipe for them. They are dense and decadent, and I can't keep myself from eating them, so I have to be careful when I make them!

An added bonus is the way your kitchen smells as these are baking. It's worth the cost of admission alone if you are a chocolate lover!

Ingredients

1 cup flour, unbleached all-purpose

1/2 cup unsweetened cocoa powder

1 teaspoon baking soda

1/4 teaspoon salt

3/4 cup heavy cream (half and half, whole milk, 2 percent, or even 1 percent can be substituted)

1 egg, beaten

2/3 cup brown sugar (dark for more flavor, light for less)

4 tablespoons salted butter, melted

2 teaspoons vanilla extract

Topping

Powdered confectioners' sugar, as needed for dusting the finished donuts

Directions

Preheat your oven to 375°F.

In a medium-sized bowl, mix the flour, cocoa powder, baking soda, and salt together until well blended.

In another bowl, mix the heavy cream, beaten egg, brown sugar, butter, and vanilla extract together.

Pour the wet ingredients into the dry, stirring until they are incorporated together.

Bake in a 375°F oven or in your donut maker for 5 to 8 minutes then remove to a cooling rack and dust immediately with powdered confectioners' sugar.

Yields 10–12 donuts.

Slow Cooker Ribs

These ribs couldn't be simpler. I like to use pork ribs, boneless and uncooked, for this, but any kind of rib you choose is fine. I love my crockpot because I can literally set it up in the morning and have ribs that night. I also enjoy smoking them, but when I've got a lot going on, this is a great way to have ribs, too!

1 pack pork ribs, boneless (2 pound pack, or close)

1 bottle favorite BBQ sauce (I like Sweet Baby Ray's Original)

Put a liner in the crockpot for easy cleanup then put the first layer of ribs in the bottom, coating with sauce and flipping over before adding more ribs. Add enough sauce to coat everything.

Set the crockpot to low heat for 7.5 hours (or 5 hours on high).

Do not, I repeat, do not take the lid off to peek until the allotted time is up. Once it is, pull the ribs out onto a plate and spoon four tablespoons of the reduced sauce on top.

Serve with fresh sauce.

We like to add mashed potatoes (Bob Evans Originals are amazing if you don't want to make your own) and green beans.

Serves 4–6 people.

Peach Crisp Crumble

L ike Jake and Suzanne, we all love peach crisp with a crumble top here, and using this recipe, it couldn't be easier! The aromas coming out of your kitchen will make you fall in love with baking all over again, and if you add a scoop of vanilla ice cream to the top when your crumble is warm, you'll be transported to those long summer days of old where the living was easy and the food so very tasty!

Ingredients

1/4 cup unsalted butter

1/2 cup flour, self-rising

1/2 cup granulated white sugar

1 teaspoon cinnamon

1/2 cup milk (whole, 2 percent, or 1 percent will do)

1 teaspoon vanilla extract

1 can peaches in heavy syrup (15 ounces or thereabouts)

Dusting of cinnamon sugar (2 tablespoons sugar to 2 teaspoons cinnamon)

Directions

Preheat the oven to 350°F.

Put the butter in a medium-sized (anything close to 8 by 8 will do) casserole dish and stick it in the oven as it is preheating.

In a medium-sized bowl, mix the flour, sugar, and cinnamon together until it is all well blended.

In the 1-cup measuring cup, add the half cup of milk and mix in the vanilla extract, then add this to the dry ingredients and stir it all together. This will make a very soupy mix, so don't be alarmed!

Remove your casserole dish carefully from the oven. It will be hot, and the butter should be mostly or all melted.

Pour in the batter first. Then open the peaches and pour it all in on top, distributing it as evenly as you can, including the heavy syrup.

DON'T mix this together. DON'T stir it. It will come out in the end, trust me.

Sprinkle the top moderately with cinnamon sugar if you wish, but this step can easily be skipped.

Bake uncovered for 45 to 50 minutes or until the top is golden brown.

Let it cool for 10 to 12 minutes, scoop out a portion, and add the ice cream if you've got it.

Enjoy!

Serves 4 to 6, or one very hungry author!

If you enjoy Jessica Beck Mysteries and you would like to be no-
tified when the next book is being released, please visit our website at
jessicabeckmysteries.net for valuable information about Jessica's books,
and sign up for her new-releases-only mail blast.

Your email address will not be shared, sold, bartered, traded, broad-
cast, or disclosed in any way. There will be no spam from us, just a
friendly reminder when the latest book is being released, and of course,
you can drop out at any time.

Other Books by Jessica Beck

The Donut Mysteries
Glazed Murder
Fatally Frosted
Sinister Sprinkles
Evil Éclairs
Tragic Toppings
Killer Crullers
Drop Dead Chocolate
Powdered Peril
Illegally Iced
Deadly Donuts
Assault and Batter
Sweet Suspects
Deep Fried Homicide
Custard Crime
Lemon Larceny
Bad Bites
Old Fashioned Crooks
Dangerous Dough
Troubled Treats
Sugar Coated Sins
Criminal Crumbs
Vanilla Vices
Raspberry Revenge
Fugitive Filling
Devil's Food Defense
Pumpkin Pleas
Floured Felonies
Mixed Malice

Tasty Trials
Baked Books
Cranberry Crimes
Boston Cream Bribes
Cherry Filled Charges
Scary Sweets
Cocoa Crush
Pastry Penalties
Apple Stuffed Alibis
Perjury Proof
Caramel Canvas
Dark Drizzles
Counterfeit Confections
Measured Mayhem
Blended Bribes
Sifted Sentences
Dusted Discoveries
Nasty Knead
Rigged Rising
Donut Despair
Whisked Warnings
Baker's Burden
Battered Bluff
The Hole Truth
Donut Disturb
Wicked Wedding Donuts
Donut Hearts Homicide
Sticky Steal
The Classic Diner Mysteries
A Chili Death
A Deadly Beef
A Killer Cake

A Baked Ham
A Bad Egg
A Real Pickle
A Burned Biscuit
The Ghost Cat Cozy Mysteries
Ghost Cat: Midnight Paws
Ghost Cat 2: Bid for Midnight
The Cast Iron Cooking Mysteries
Cast Iron Will
Cast Iron Conviction
Cast Iron Alibi
Cast Iron Motive
Cast Iron Suspicion
Nonfiction
The Donut Mysteries Cookbook

Made in the USA
Middletown, DE
11 February 2023

24385563R00116